SHE

Tales

of

Womyn

Cover Design by Wayne Allen Jones

The photograph used for the cover and title page shows an ancient sculptural vulvaform petroglyph and was taken by Hart W. Empie. It appears in *Minding a Sacred Place* written by Hart W. and Sunnie Empie. (2001)

The universal symbolism of the vulvaform celebrates the Goddess-Creatrix, our Mother Earth, and the fecundity, fertility, and creative abundance of the feminine life force. This 8' by 4' prehistoric granite imagery was carved millennia ago (possibly 5,000 to 7,000 years) by our American Indian ancestors at a site in what is now Carefree, Arizona in the magnificent high Sonoran Desert. The Empie Petroglyph Site is on the national Registry of Historic Places.

Similar symbolic representations of the vulva are found throughout the world, some dating as far back as 30,000 years. Matricentric societies that honored the feminine generative nature occurred in numerous and independent cultures worldwide. According to psychologist Carl Jung, these symbols are evidence of the "collective unconscious" memories of our shared primordial past and are an integral part of each of us.

SHE

Tales
of
Womyn

Maureen Jones-Ryan

COPYRIGHT © 2005 BY MAUREEN JONES-RYAN

All rights reserved. No part of this work may be reproduced or transmitted in any format by any means, electronic or mechanical, including photocopying and recording, or by any information storage or retrieval system, without written permission from the author, except by a reviewer.

Published by FRACTAL EDGE PRESS
PO Box 220586, Chicago, IL 60622-0586
E-mail: FEPedit@FractalEdgePress.com
Website: www.FractalEdgePress.com
Phone: 773-793-4095

Printed in the United States of America by:
CGA: Corporate Graphics of America
5312 N. Elston Avenue, Chicago, IL 60630
Phone: 773-481-2100
E-mail: cgaprint@sbcglobal.net
Website: www.printcga.com

Book design: Wayne Allen Jones
Cover photo: Hart W. Empie
  Digitally modified by Wayne Allen Jones
Author photo: Bob Ryan

Title text: Imprint MT Shadow
Body text: Book Antiqua 10pt.
Printed on archival-quality, acid-free paper

FIRST EDITION
Distributed in Chicago by:
The Puddin'head Press
PO Box 477889, Chicago, IL 60647-7889
Phone: 1888-BOOKS-98

ISBN 1-933126-20-5   15.00

Dedication

To girls and womyn throughout the world
whose stories are innumerable, inseparable,
and inspirational.

To Rosalind
who took on the education of Orlando
knowing there is never too much of a good thing.

To Bob
who taught me, indeed,
there is never too much of a good thing.

To Ophelia
Who *was the more deceived.*

To Emily, *Of whom so dear*
The name to hear
Illumines with a Glow
As intimate – as fugitive
As Sunset on the snow.

To Frida who taught me to write
My own reality.

and

To all poets and short story writers and their readers
throughout the world
who know that each day in every life is a personal collection
of poetic short stories.

Seldom, very seldom does complete truth belong to any human disclosure; seldom can it happen that something is not a little disguised, or a little mistaken.
Jane Austen, *Emma*

I am always at a loss to know how much to believe of my own stories.
Washington Irving *Tales of a Traveler (1824)*

ALSO BY MAUREEN JONES-RYAN

Books
Meditation Without Frills, Schenkman Publishers, 1975
Thirty-Three and Mortgage Free, Schenkman Publishers, 1977
Colorful Seasons of Arizona, Carlos Elmer Publishing, 1978
An Arizona Christmas, Carlos Elmer Publishing, 1979
Square Blue Moons, Harold Douglas Press, 1982
The Scarlet Letter (with D. Sanche), Harold Douglas Press, 1984

Edited Collections
The M-Muse (editor)
The Worcester Poetess (editor)
Top Shelf Reviews (editor)

Works in Process
Thicker Than Blood: Friendships Between and Among Womyn
Frida Kahlo: Art as Autobiography

Preface

There are only two or three human stories, and they go on repeating themselves as fiercely as if they had never happened before.
      Willa Sibert Cather, *O Pioneers!* (1913)

  The short story is a glimpse – a mere snippet – into a moment in a life. While the characters and events named in the following short stories are inventions of my imagination, they are not fictitious. There is no such thing as fiction.

  Way back in the previous century, while studying existential phenomenological psychology under the tutelage of Dr. Frank Buckley, my suspicions were confirmed that fiction simply does not exist. All stories, all characters, all thoughts and feelings exist somewhere in the history of our Universe; somewhere in the being of womyn, of man; somewhere in the heart, mind, and soul of each of us.

  And so, the following short stories are existential truths drawn from my Universal Consciousness. My Universal Memory. My Universal Imagination. They may be your stories. They may belong to someone you know. Or they may belong to someone you will know. Regardless, the truths of the stories and characters are there.

  They are not fictitious. There is no such thing as fiction.

About the Author

Tolstoy was talking as much about writers as he was about families when he said in *Anna Karenina:* "Happy families are all alike; every unhappy family is unhappy in its own way." Writers are all alike; made both happy and miserable by their writing. The author's happiness is born of her writing and her unhappiness is spawned from the same womb.

Dr. Maureen Jones-Ryan holds two doctorate degrees: an earned Ph.D. in the Psychology of Womyn and an honorary Litt.D. in Comparative World Literatures with a specialty in Womyn in Holy Literatures. Her profession is feminist psychology; her avocations are poetry and comparative world religions.

Maureen is founder of the International Sexual Abuse and Domestic Violence Memorial; president of the Sexual Assault Recovery Institute; serves on several non-profit and for-profit boards of directors; Founder of and Spiritual Director for Universal Spirit Quest, a non-sectarian congregation; a political and social activist; a reader, writer, poet, gardener, and friend.

She is currently working on a biography of Frida Kahlo. Pending publication is her book on sorology[§], *Thicker Than Blood: Friendships Between and Among Womyn.*

While her addresses are Arizona and Campbello Island, New Brunswick, her home is the Universe.

[§] Sorology – from the Greek *soro* for sister and *ology* for the study of – is a newly coined word identifying the study of friendships between and among womyn; a subject that has been ignored, neglected, dismissed, and discredited over the centuries in literature, histories, religions, academics, psychology, philosophy, medicine, and sociology.

Contents

Pyracantha	1
Janelle	6
Margeena	10
Her Holiness	14
Frida	18
Beth	25
The Old Womyn[§]	30
Faith	31
Rosalind	38
Mrs. Rousseau	45
Nora	52
Polly	61
Carnival	65
The Offender	69
Moonpath	76
Aristotle	80
Emily	87
Maria	92
Elefantina	97
Consummation	102
Olive	106
Readers' Guide: Questions for Discussion Groups	111

[§]Womyn is the alternative spelling of woman and women. Included in the *Random House Dictionary,* it is widely used by writers who wish to accentuate the uniqueness of womyn.

Pyracantha

She stood naked in the shower. It was a cramped, white tiled stall with a smoked, nubby-glassed door that steamed up when she let the hot water run. On the steamy door she enjoyed writing favorite words with her finger. She loved words. She made them her secret conspirators against the others. Sometimes she would write the same word over and over again in varying scripts; squiggly, plain, cursive, block print. Strong words when she needed their strength. Soft words when she needed their calming influence. Soaring words when she felt ecstatic. Like the day she received notice her Fulbright application had been accepted. *Ecclesiastical. Labialization. Rondeau Redouble. Syncopation.* She soared with them.

Today she didn't need words. She felt strong and calm and ecstatic all at once. She needed to decide only the minor, last minute logistics. How best to execute the plan. The one-sided razor she held lightly in her right hand. She had bought it four days ago. It had come in a package of four, and she carefully selected one, throwing the remaining three in the trash. She could have put them in his drawer with his others, but she didn't for the same reason she had not used one of his. This act was hers. She wanted to share none of it with others, especially him. She did not want him, later, to feel he'd been any part of it.

But how to do it? If she turned on the shower, the razor may become slippery and difficult to hold firmly. If she did not turn it on, the blood would not wash away. She wanted no blood left behind. Her blood was hers only. Private. Warm. Personal. She wouldn't allow them to find it dry, cold, and lifeless painted on the white tiles. She would make sure it would wash cleanly down the drain, into the septic and become part of the Earth. The pyracantha she had planted two years ago by the septic would be nurtured – if no longer by her hand – by her blood. Systemically.

She wondered if blood continued to drain from a lifeless body. She would prefer all of it to drain away to her pyracantha. She decided, however, that once blood pressure dropped, the blood would no longer flow through the veins and arteries to the freedom her razor would provide. No matter, her bushes would receive several pints, maybe more.

There was no need for a note. What would she say that had not been said at some point in their 20 years together? A note would be no more clarifying nor illuminating for him than had been her words. Everything had been done. Everything had been said.

He understood she loved him. Of this she was gratefully aware. Somewhere in the gentle, green hills of his mind, he knew her Love for him existed, but he could never seem to reach it: to touch it or be heard by it. Her Love was like a vague shadow ahead of him in the mist. As in his childhood dreams, he called to it, hurried after it, but it remained just beyond his reach. Always with a not-quite-identifiable form. Occasionally, over the years, it would turn a sudden corner – always to the left – and, for a time, be out of his sight. This only increased the intensity of his pursuit. He was never sure if, when the Love was again discernible, he had caught up with it, or it had found him.

She understood his need. She also understood she was incapable of soothing it for more than short periods at a time. This saddened her. In their early years together she was determined to try. Until then she thought it impossible for her to control the omnipresent Green Fire that was her spirit. Sometimes it would abate, but never quite be extinguished. Always smoldering. A constant reminder of its power to erupt into the savagery of anger or the passion of action.

Then they were together and the raging Green Flames were (for a time) tamed. How naïve she had been to believe her love for him would, or even could, supplant the Fire; or, at least, satisfy the hunger of the Flames. No. She knew better now. Red flames, blue flames, even white flames had limited appetites. The Green Flame was insatiable. If its appetite were simply carnal, it would have been appeased by their togetherness.

And so, residing within her these twenty years were the two central and life sustaining elements of her being; the intense and unwavering Love for him and the quenchless Green Fire. They were, at best, uneasy neighbors; at worst, warring, carnivorous, carnage mongers.

She was several years into the marriage before accepting the truth; the two primary elements were in no way related – not even similar. What satisfied one invoked violent jealousy in the other. Her twenty years with him were marked by an incessant struggle to maintain a balance between the two. To satisfy the appetites of both without incurring the wrath of either. Unquestionable was her conscious and sub-conscious awareness that without both, her life would end.

"Perhaps," she often thought, "if I'd been born a Libra instead of a Virgo my struggle with balance would be less futile."

The Fire left her quietly but surely. Now, looking back, she knows the precise moment of its departure. At the time she had thought it had simply ebbed. But that was over a year ago. She had been left with only the Love for him in a body without life, in a life without Fire.

Its appetite had become increasingly more inventive. When once it was satisfied with minor scraps of cultural and spiritual diversions, it quickly grew more demanding and at the same time more discriminating. Vicarious intellectual pursuits soon evolved into a desire to consume tangible, substantive experiences. Until, finally, she had to deny its most ambitious desire.

The Fulbright Fellowship was for three years in India. The Fire pined for it. Pleaded with her. Reasoned. Rationalized. Alternated between angry vituperation and cunning cajolery. For months the Love and the raging Green Fire battled within her.

The deadline for her decision arrived. She sat to write her letter of acceptance or rejection not knowing, even then, which it would be. Her pen moved across the paper, and she realized the Love for him was guiding her hand.

The Green Fire was never felt again. At first relief. She could live without it, in peace for the first time. But, no. She was out of balance. Out of life. Cold.

Just as the Love had inflamed the Green Fire, so had the Fire warmed the Love.

He felt it, sensed it, was pained by it as soon as it happened. From his insecurity he construed it as the death of the Love for him. How could she explain that it was from the Love's strength, its power, the inevitable, definitive battle had been waged, and the Love was the vanquisher?

She turned on the shower. Warm. Soothing. Arms at her side, careful not to let the razor nick her thigh, she lifted her face to the spray. It gently cascaded over her head, her shoulders, down her back and front to her feet. How delicious it was. How sensuous. (This was another word she loved which she was careful to distinguish from "sensual," which she never wrote in the steam.)

She thought again, as she had frequently in the past few months, of Claudio's speech to his sister, in *Measure for Measure:*

> Ay, but to die, and go we know not where;
> To lie in cold obstruction and to rot;
> This sensible warm notion to become
> A kneaded clod; and the delighted spirit
> To bathe in fiery floods, or to reside
> In thrilling region of thick-ribbed ice,
> To be imprison'd in the viewless winds
> And blown with restless violence round about
> The pendent world; or to be worse than worst
> Of those that lawless and incertain thought
> Imagine howling! 'Tis too horrible!
> The weariest and most loathed worldly life
> That age, ache, penury, and imprisonment
> Can lay on nature is a paradise
> To what we fear of death.

How wrong he was. How lacking in insight. Age, ache, penury or imprisonment are nothing compared to the loss of the Fire. It may be possible to continue a form of life after the loss of red, blue, or even white fire. But those few who know the Green Fire understand that life ends with its demise. Obviously Claudio was not counted among those few blessed (or was it cursed?) with the Green Fire for his soul.

And what is there to fear of death? It is birth one should fear. The beginning of the journey holds so much of the unknown. The conclusion of the journey finds all placed behind you. There is no more. There is only nothingness. Of nothingness there is no fear.

She curled up on the floor, amused by the irony that the cramped cubicle necessitated her assuming the fetal position. Her left arm outstretched, her head on its biceps, she was careful to leave the drain clear.

He would cry, she knew. He would mourn in ever-receding levels of his consciousness, perhaps forever. But, in the fertile, gentle greenness of his mind, he would understand, if not at once, this act was her final test and expression of the Love. He, too, must be saved from days, months, years of life with a lover without the Fire; any fire. Even a life with a womyn blessed only with red fire was better than enduring time with a loved one who had, and lost, the Green Fire.

She firmly sank the blade into her left wrist. The flow was immediate and steady; it homogenized with the shower water and swirled down the drain.

Gently, without moving her left hand from its position over the drain, she placed the razor on the doorstep – to the far side so no one would cut themselves.

Before returning her hand to a comfortable position under her chin, she traced in the steam, on the bottom of the door, one last, lovely word: *pyracantha.*

JANELLE

She was uncomfortable with this one: childlike, vulnerable and, most discomfiting of all, transparent. Her name fitted her presence: Angel. Angel Gonzales. Her brown satin skin, large ivory teeth, and raven hair shone with the health of a womyn in touch with nature. Then there were her eyes.

Janelle later tried to remember what color they were; she found herself vacillating between pale blue and black. Regardless of the color, they were like no eyes she had ever experienced. They were disturbing in a way that attracted rather than repelled, yet Janelle, who encouraged her patients to (and prided herself on) look everyone with whom you spoke in the eyes, was unable to maintain unswerving contact with Angel's eyes. No sooner would she look away, however, than she was compelled to seek them out again.

She had no idea how many rape and incest victims she had treated in her thirty-two years. Certainly over a thousand and maybe closer to two. A rainbow of girls and womyn brave enough to look pain in the eye and make it blink. Womyn with courage and fear and self-confidence and self-loathing and, above all, a desperate determination to repossess their lives. She thought of them with respect and affection and wondered where life had taken them and where they had taken life.

Some had remained in touch over the years: an occasional letter or card with words of love and appreciation. Pictures of their children or an invitation to their college graduations. She always was warmed by their expressions of gratitude – frequently somewhat hyperbolic – for "saving my life." She knew she had not saved any lives; only guided them toward the discovery they could save their own.

Thirty-two years in the same institution. She was only 24 when she applied for the job. Twenty-four; the ink not dry on her Masters Degree; and full of – as her mother would say – piss 'n vinegar. Where had the time gone? Where had the piss 'n vinegar gone? And in all those years and through the thousands and thousands of patient interviews, she had never felt as disturbed by – and at the same time attracted to – a new patient as she did with Angel Gonzales.

Ordinarily she would not have done the in-take interview, but it was the holidays and several of her therapists were off work.

"Come in, Ms. Gonzales," she had greeted her, "I'm Dr. Buckley." She smiled and motioned to the chair across from her own. "Please make yourself comfortable."

She was always careful to maintain a veil of professional distance between herself and her patients. "I am not your friend," she would remind them, "I am your psychotherapist." (She always smiled when she recalled Macia; a former patient with piss 'n vinegar to spare. "I hope that's not two words, Dr. Buckley." Now *there* was a womyn with wit! – and maybe insight?) She never invited patients to use her first name. "Dr." was part of the fabric of separation upon which she insisted. A membrane of hard-fought for letters.

What impressed her first was Angel's quiet self-confidence. Most womyn, upon entering her office for the first time, were tense, anxious, and often tearful. They were rarely able to look her in the eye and were often defensive and distrustful. She treated only FASI's – Female Adult Survivors of Incest – and expected new patients to need reassurance that they were in a safe place and their confidentiality would be respected.

Angel, however, was unlike any patient she had ever interviewed. She spoke quietly: not quite *sotto voce,* but softly enough to demand Janelle's close attention. Her presence was calm and serene as she told Janelle why she had asked to see her. "When I called to make an appointment to see you, Dr. Buckley, I was told you did not do in-take appointments, but somehow I knew it would be you who would interview me." She smiled as her eyes – indeed, her entire essence – embraced Janelle.

Janelle returned her smile but made no comment. She was already beginning to feel a most unusual sense of fascination with this womyn who sat comfortably across from her.

"I saw you on the television [use of the article gave her diction a softly archaic air] talking about survivors of incest," Angel continued, "and I felt compelled to call." She paused, her hands quietly resting in her lap, and gazed gently but steadily at Janelle.

Expecting her to continue, Janelle waited a moment before clearing her throat. "Were you sexually abused in childhood?" she asked. It was always best to ask the question directly; the question that may never have been asked of them before – perhaps even of themselves.

"Haven't all womyn been sexually abused to one degree or another?" She smiled – a sweet, almost innocent smile that radiated warmth throughout the room. "My older sister's husband died three months ago. In all probability, he is suffering now for what he did to me when I was a little girl. I never told anyone until now."

Janelle felt Angel's eyes watching her as she made notes on the in-take form. When she looked up she could not resist being drawn into the black – or was it pale blue – pool that seemed to engulf her. She was surrounded – or so she thought – by a comforting warmth and light that was neither tangible nor quantifiable, but was unequivocal. The two womyn smiled at each other and sat in comfortable silence for what seemed eternity.

"When you were sexually abused, Dr. Buckley, did you tell anyone?" The pool of Angel's eyes continued to embrace Janelle with comforting warmth.

Thirty-two years and untold thousands of hours talking with womyn; womyn who were bruised, hurt, damaged, and wounded. Womyn who turned to her to help them out of the depressive, destructive, and obstructionist morass of victim and into the liberty and justice (for all) of survivor. Womyn who loved and trusted her. And at least half of those womyn had asked, either directly or vicariously, if she herself had been sexually abused.

Always her answer was the same: elusive, enigmatic, and discouraging of further enquiry; "I'm a feminist committed to assisting my sisters out of their pain and into their power. Whether or not I've been sexually abused neither enhances nor facilitates my mission, or your goal of recovery." Her answer, though intentionally obscure, was always delivered gently but firmly and never did the same womyn inquire twice. ["I am not your friend. I am your psychotherapist."]

And now – here in front of her – was this numinous womyn – a womyn on whom she had not set eyes more than an hour ago – moving beyond enquiry to *knowing.*

It never even occurred to Janelle – never crossed her mind – to offer her standard reply. How could she? The question was not the standard question, nor was it posed by a standard patient. The melting of her long-held professional reserve bathed her in a sensuous lightness of being. Along with her eyes, Janelle lowered her voice. "No." She lifted her eyes and re-entered the pool. "No, I never told anyone until now."

Angel did not move from her chair, but Janelle felt enveloped by her compassion. It washed over her in liquid waves of lavender, luminosity, and love. She was relaxed and weightless. She wanted to laugh and cry and laugh some more. Instead she stood up signaling the end of the interview. "I'll look forward to seeing you at therapy group on Thursday."

~~ : ~~

The Thursday group meeting was crowded. When Janelle entered the room she was greeted warmly by the womyn. "Hi, Dr. Buckley." "Hey, you look great tonight." "Gosh, Dr. Buckley, you look different somehow. Have you changed your hair or something?" She looked around the small room and was not surprised at Angel's absence.

"Tonight," she began, "I would like to introduce a new member to the group and, if you don't mind, let her begin the session by sharing her story." The womyn looked curiously around the room and not seeing any new member present, looked inquisitively at Dr. Buckley.

"My name is Janelle," she said, "and in addition to being your therapist, I would like to be your friend."

Margeena

She had never felt such an aching need for her mother before she was about to be hysterectomized. The yearning was physical: not the customary ache she had accepted as chronic since Mother's death three years previous, but a somatic and tangible pain. The throe began with a low and mournful keening rising up from her uterus. She could hear the mournful dirge reverberate through her body as the intensity of sonance swelled to a torturous, spirit-shattering cacophony. The waves of agony overwhelmed her until she was overcome with a deluge of grief that left her emotionally spent and physically exhausted.

Mother had died on Mothers' Day, a curious coincidence as her own mother – Nana – had also died on Mothers' Day forty years previous. Both womyn lived 89 years in the same small New England town.

In Mother's memory, Margeena planted a yellow rose bush in her hill-side garden. Yellow roses were always Mother's favorite. "They bring me back to my girlhood," she would say, but would explain no more. It saddened Margeena that, despite tender loving care, the rose bush never thrived.

Margeena often wondered about Mother's girlhood: grand mal epileptic seizures since birth and deafened by scarlet fever at eight, she was raised with the shame of the era attached to both conditions. It was a well-known fact that epileptics were possessed by the devil, and the deaf were most likely retarded. Despite – or perhaps because of – her triple handicaps: epilepsy, deafness, and shame, Mother immersed herself in books and acquired a liberal education whose depth and breadth surpassed that of most of today's college graduates. She was, Margeena thought, a pre-feminist feminist.

It was Mother who had lovingly and naturally introduced Margeena to her uterus. During the first half of the last century she had been, as was her mother before her, the womyn to whom neighbors and family in their rural community turned for advice for themselves and instruction for their daughters in the magic and mystery of womynhood. She guided innumerable girls and womyn toward an understanding of their feminine powers, while sharing the secrets of how to create babies and how to prevent them from being created.

Mother possessed a unique and extraordinary sagacity: a rare ability to communicate. "Mother," – Margeena always called her Mother – "how have you learned so much? There is nothing you don't understand."

Mother would throw back her head and laugh that singular laugh of the deaf. She explained that when she was given the choice of listening to the clamorous racket of the world or the wisdom of the goddesses, she chose the latter. Margeena believed her and drank from her meniscus-brimmed cup of wisdom in hopes of acquiring Mother's gentle feminism.

It was from Mother, then, that Margeena learned the power and possibilities of her uterus: the knowledge, energy, memory, and magic residing deep within her life-giving darkness. It was from Mother she learned to celebrate this essence of womynhood that encompasses far more than conception and childbirth.

While others whole-*heartedly* committed to projects, Margeena commended her whole uterus. It was her uterus that broke when she failed, and she cried not her heart out but her uterus out in frustration. It was her uterus that ached when she felt compassion and her uterus that throbbed with love for her sweetheart.

Her life's work was with womyn who had been traumatized by sexual abuse. For many of her patients, the burden of pain was overwhelming, destructive, and obstructive to healing. Their healing could only begin when the burden of pain was lightened. She perceived her role, for the past thirty years, as attempting to relieve the encumbrance of their pain by acknowledging it, embracing it, and absorbing it into her own womb. By lifting their pain she knew it would allow the survivors an opportunity to regenerate their own uterine energies and shed their uterine despair.

Margeena rejoiced as she witnessed her patients renew their spirits; those beau ideal feminine spirits that had been so brutally ruptured by sexual abuse. She knew her uterus was up to the challenge: She was strong and she was willing.

And then her uterus sent her the message she knew would come some day – but, ah, so soon? She would no longer expel her wondrous monthly nectar. Her menses would pause as she graduated to the next station in her womynhood: She and her uterus had earned the station of Crone.

It was with affection and gratitude Margeena experienced the changes in her uterine activity. Their relationship, as partners in the healing of others, would only strengthen as the years progressed. It was time for her uterus to enjoy a well-earned rest.

It was not long, however, before her uterus began relaying messages of greater urgency. She was four times her normal size and harboring unfriendly growths throughout and beyond. It was time for them to separate – but only physically. Margeena was determined they would carry on their healing and nurturing work apart from each other, sustained by the strength acquired from fifty years of mutual succorance, sustenance, and support. Their bodies would no longer be physically connected, but their spirits . . . ah, their spirit was One and Everlasting.

Edna St. Vincent Millay spoke of Margeena when she confessed:

My candle burns at both ends:
It will not last the night;
But, ah, my foes, and, oh, my friends –
It gives a lovely light.

Such was the power and force of her uterine energy fostered throughout the years, her light would *not* extinguish but would be transformed, transpicuous, and transcendent. Her spirit was now to warm rather than burn; to radiate rather than pierce; to glow rather than explode.

Through years of uterine nurturing, Margeena was well prepared for her second fifty years. Her gentler, more quintessentially female light *would* last the night. Her work would continue in a more tranquil but powerfully thaumaturgic manner. Such is the essence of Crone.

What would happen, Margeena worried, to her partner of 50 years; her womb, her muse, her creator, her matriarch? She would not allow her to be disposed of in a medical trash incinerator. She must be cared for as lovingly as she had cared for Margeena these past fifty years. And, if possible, to continue her work of nurturing even in her incorporeal state.

The protracted hospital stay was over at last. She would be discharged and sent home tomorrow, and she would be accompanied by, despite some initial objections of officious hospital administrators, her life-long companion, her uterus.

The solitary ceremony took place in her hill-side garden. As Margeena reverently lowered her uterus into the ground beneath Mother's yellow rose bush, Edna again offered her words:

Into the darkness they go, the wise and the lovely. Crowned With lilies and with laurel they go; but I am not resigned.

The earth is warm where she rests and not a day goes by Margeena does not think of her. As the spirit of her Crone evolves, she has never felt closer to her uterus or to Mother.

Mother's yellow rose bush has suddenly come to life. The blooms are prodigious and ubiquitous. They perfume the yard with the sensuous aroma of fecundity and banish the mournful keening of loss. In its place is the music of Mother throwing back her head and laughing with the goddesses.

Her Holiness

She was a womyn who had departed time and space. The dead grey of her foggy, unfocused eyes – those funereal orbs – looked neither outward nor inward; the physicality of her universe and the spirituality of her soul no longer existed.

Tilly's Bar. She was born in the satanic booth in which she slumped into her communion chalice of gin sans tonic. Born of the splintered, mildewed wood and faded, chipped formica; nurtured by the smoke-saturated air that orchestrated the phlegm-spewing, hacking coughs in that dank and stinking corner of her temple cum church cum office cum sarcophagus known as Tilly's.

It is to this ancient altar the rummy-eyed masses flock for her blessings: the holy service of her Mass – that ancient rite of cleansing and release – offered 24/7. No sermons. No building fund appeals. No confession of sins. Baptism not required if you're a confirmed, certified (or certifiable) resident of Hell seeking only the post-extreme unction of the damned.

And so they come each day (or night): 3, 6, 9 or none to this Priestess of Tilly's (thank god for Saint Tilly!) with their sacramental juices to be silently offered – sacrificed – at her altar. Two dollars or a quarter the devout supplicate before Her Holiness – their offering assuring the up-keep of her blessed communion Chalice. And the incense of her putrid body washes over them mingling with their own pukka stench of the soul-less (or soul-full) damned.

Her Holiness – the dead and damned priestess of Tilly's – knew well her congregation. Shuffling with each in turn to the back room – that most sanctified of inner-sanctums – each five-minute Mass customized to comfort the comfortless.

Solemn, dreadlocked Professor who slept on the steps of the shelter down the street, clutching his sack of books, refusing to go inside in the hottest and coldest of weather. His Mass was longer than most: he wanted only to read to her as she slept naked on the soggy, filthy mattress stained with body fluids from the natural and unnatural orifices of innumerable bodies – hundreds maybe thousands of bodies. Black, yellow, brown, white, gray, red, green each embracing the mattress that claimed the better part of the concrete floor in this *sanctum sanctorum*. Each leaves his own mark and stench and memory.

The deranged and dumb Jew (whose voice she never knew) ravenously biting into her bony buttocks creating a palette of bruises but not often drawing blood. The blind, toothless, octogenarian Adolph who worshiped daily, cradled in the arms of our priestess while gumming her bitter, brown teats that hung from the skin of those empty and deflated bags that once were her breasts. The misogamist, William ("Never, never call me Bill"), whose worship was often interrupted by the morose bartender pounding on the door, "Keep yer fuk'n noise down in there!" (William worshiped his own hatred of womyn – all womyn – with foreplay of shouted obscenities). Nicholas, the quiet Greek who once – was it days or years ago? – bartered a quarter-full bottle of Channel #5 for her blessings. (She put it to its best possible use: to top off her Chalice with the fragrance of the stars.) Three hundred pound Charlie singing the Lord's Prayer while urinating on her filthy, black, and bony feet: his prayers complete, he fastidiously dries her with his tattered shirt tails, kisses her on her sunken, pock-marked face, and leaves: the parade of prayerful worshippers continues. They seep into the church of the unredeemed in their fetid togs held up by ropes, held together by rusty pins; stained by the body's holy waters: urine, blood, vomit, feces, semen, and snot. And the high priestess dispenses her benedictions, and the meniscus of her Holy Grail diminishes not.

Pre-ordination our heroine did things: her hair, laundry, beds in a motel around the corner from her walk-up flat, and her then clean nails. She did life – on the lowest rung perhaps, but life none-the-less. And then life did her, and she graduated from motel maid to soul-less priestess of the lost.

The maid knew no Shabbat. The priestess celebrates seven Sabbaths a week.

The maid's theology was pictorially detailed (angels, harps, golden gates – conversely, fire, demons, and three pronged prods); the priestess' inner screen is dark, black, and soundless – her personal projectionist dead in the projection booth.

(What becomes of a soul that predeceases its body?)

It is Tuesday at two in this decrepit but holy sanctuary across from the equally decrepit but unholy Veterans Administration Hospital that dispenses neither sanctuary nor sanity. She is vaguely aware of his cursing as he wrestles his battered wheelchair through Saint Tilly's door. He rolls to the bar. Morose Bartender wordlessly pours and hands him his usual (scotch with a beer chaser) and silently resumes his mindless staring at the 6" television secured behind and under the bar.

"Sorry I can't linger to enjoy your scintillating conversation," he booms, "but I can't keep my date waiting." He chuckles as he rolls toward Her Holiness.

"Fuck you," mumbles Morose Barkeep. He was accustomed to this rolling soul's caustic commentary.

Her Holiness watched as he rolled toward her. Her bleary, dead eyes suddenly came alive with something that resembled interest. Wordlessly she stood, gulped down the remainder of her Chalice and silently observed him.

"Are we ready?" He spoke softly, unlike his usual booming bluster.

For a moment the frozen death of her face softened with gratitude; he heard her soundless expression and understood. Taking her nicotine-stained yellow, dirty black, and bruised blue hand in his, he rolled toward the entrance of the inner sanctum where she kneeled in front of him in that age old position of grace.

His hands cupped her face as he turned it up toward him. No longer a death mask, it shone with the innocence of a girl, the joy and wonder of the redeemed. Her sweetness took his breath away as tears streamed down his upper cheek to be caught in the matted and grimy mass of his beard. "You are beautiful," he sighed. "Your time is up in Hell, Sweet Angel. Time to head for Heaven. You've sure as hell paid your way."

He gently pushed her head toward his crotch and groaned softly throughout her Mass. Post-communion, she wiped her mouth on his pant leg and remained humbly kneeling before him slumped back on her heels. He smiled his gratitude for her last holy act as she tenderly tucked his now limp flesh into his soiled pants.

"Maybe I'll see you there some day, but for now I'll simply transfer one Hell for another. Prison or that damned VA hospital. Makes little difference to me." His voice was light and clean: decisive. He spoke to her eyes that were – for the first time since he joined her congregation – clear and shining. The fog that had resided behind them was lifted and their color – rich brown – startled him.

He withdrew the gun from where it was tucked beside him on his chair. She stroked it lovingly for a brief moment before kissing his hands – first one then the other. She rose up straight and proud on her knees, folded her hands around his, which now embraced the warm metal, and slowly – almost sensuously – slid the barrel into her mouth. Her chin rose slightly toward her destination, she serenely closed her eyes.

He delivered his gift to her without hesitation. As he patiently awaited transport to his new Hell, he blessed her liquefied brains, blood, and flesh which had already transuded into the mattress to blend with the other souls there memorialized.

Frida

She held the ornate silver mirror in her left hand and extended her arm so her entire face and long, graceful neck were reflected. She was proud of her neck; white, slender, and swanlike: she dressed to show it to advantage. In her right hand she held an immaculately clean, sable brush with which she gently touched the virgin canvas.

The translucent light of the Mexican winter filtered through the delicate, rhythmically breathing lace curtains at the open window. The gentle air that gave breath to the lace was perfumed by sweet desert rains and tasted of bougainvillea and Palo Verde. Lying flat on her back with but one pillow under her head and a second under her knees, she forgot for a moment her pain as she examined the image in the mirror: high, creaseless forehead made prominent by severely swept back, jet hair in two plaits that coiled softly on either side of her head – sensuous black snakes with bright red ribbons flirtatiously bowed on their tails; large ears with full lobes unpunctured by cosmetic needles; classically large, straight nose proudly separating penetratingly black, almond eyes that stared unflinchingly through the present to the past and future – they held no truck with prevarication (her own or others); unsmiling mouth (bordering on grim) unselfconsciously tucked under the softest whisper of a feminine mustache; and, dominating center stage, the dramatic sweep of a single eyebrow writ large – a black-winged bird flying courageously into the world.

The massive four-poster bed – masculine in its dark, ornately carved wooden beams – had a full length mirror on the underside of the wooden canopy. How many hours – hundreds, thousands – had she scrutinized her broken, pain-racked body, as she lay alone and lonely awaiting his attendance. Within easy reach was a table upon which, neatly arranged, were her tools of transport to both her inner life and the life beyond her bed-cum-prison: paints, brushes, books, pens, and stationary.

The hand-held mirror allowed her to examine her face more closely with the tender intimacy of a mother gazing at the face of her newborn. The reflection in the full length canopy mirror – always there – became her second self. Or was the Frida in the canopy the original, making the twisted and scarred body beneath the reflected Frida?

Two mirrors. Two Fridas. Perhaps the twisted deformities of her canopy body were simply due to parallax error?

The first spot of paint on her canvas was always some shade of red – blood red – which breathed life into the canvas and broke the hymenic barrier to her creativity allowing the conception of her mind's child. Today the blood seeped from her brush onto the center of the canvas where, this time, she would give birth to herself. Unlike most of her paintings, the image of her self-birthing had not come to her as an epiphany but, rather, as a slowly maturing realization that she was her mother and her mother was herself. (Had she but known that the eventual caretaker of her Birth would be the yet-unborn brilliant American entertainer named – most appropriately – Madonna, she would have been pleased.)

The canvas thus initiated to life with the first blood-red pangs of labor, she released her breath, which she had been holding for longer than she knew. Slowly lowering the hand mirror onto the pristine white sheets upon which she reclined, she carefully cleaned the red-tipped brush and gently placed it with the others in the wooden palette box. She sighed as she closed the cover. She could not paint today. Not today. She would wait for the hour of his arrival and, until then, gather her thoughts and strength for the inevitable confrontation ahead.

She would get out of bed and into her wheel chair for his visit. But first she must decide how to dress. The tortoise-shell earrings in the shape of tiny hands with gold cuffs given her by Picasso in 1939 she would certainly wear. (Could it possibly be fifteen years since her trip to Paris? Where had her life gone in that time?) And one of her beautifully embroidered Tehuana blouses with the traditional long purple velvet skirt with a white cotton ruffle at the hem: Diego liked the Tehuana costume worn by womyn of the isthmus purported to be the most beautiful, sensuous, intelligent, brave, and strongest womyn of Mexico. It was alleged the Tehuantepec womyn rigorously maintained a matriarchal society in which they directed the market, managed all financial matters, and governed the men. It was also rumored that one of Diego's many infidelities was with a Tehuana womyn of legendary beauty. (She had forgiven him his many peccadilloes, but this time it would take far greater effort for forgiveness to heal her heart and her marriage.)

Her clothes were a fourth language for her in which she was more fluent than most. Her remarkable self-confidence and self-image were always expressed in her exotic and quixotic wardrobe. As pride in her *Mexicanidad* identity grew, she dressed almost exclusively in traditional Mexican costumes from various periods, regions, and social classes: she always painted herself thus attired.

The door opened, and her nurse entered: a proud womyn who allowed her Indian blood to course through every gesture, glance, and word. "I want to get dressed and into my chair. Señor Rivera will be here soon."

"But Señorita," Nurse Mayet looked troubled. "You are so tired. Wouldn't it be best to receive him in bed?" She didn't expect an answer as she quietly proceeded to assist Frida out of bed. She was only too aware of the futility of arguing with her patient. Her "tsk tsks" were met with Frida's solemn smile. "We don't have to worry about doing my hair. I'm going to wear my headdress."

Since the accident, now almost thirty years ago, Señora Mayet nursed Frida through the innumerable surgeries, marital complexities, love affairs, and mercurial moods. They were the same age then as they were now, however their relationship, though intimate, maintained a veneer of formality. Perhaps more than any other person, Frida trusted and depended upon this simple womyn who had become an integral part of her household. She was fiercely loyal and ferocious in her protection of Frida's privacy, many secrets, and well-being. Despite Frida's marital state, Señora Mayet continued to call her Señorita.

Señora Mayet took from the large armoire the elaborate headdress. Of heavily starched lace pleats, it was reminiscent of an oversized Elizabethan ruff and was worn by Tehuana womyn on special occasions. "Surely," she thought, "this is a special occasion." She chuckled to herself as Señora Mayet's "tsk tsks" increased in volume and number.

Frida's Mexicanism was proclaimed by her manner of dress as surely as her Communism was proclaimed by her political activism. Her Hungarian-Jewish agnate heritage was not denied, but simply overwhelmed by her near fanatical identification with the people of her homeland and rejection of foreign classism, most particularly American and French bureaucracies and elitism. Her rejection of bourgeois social conformity was vociferously expressed by her uniquely dramatic – some thought bizarre – fashion.

"I'll wear my boots." Señora Mayet brought the short leather boots that she invariably selected to wear whenever she expected to spend serious time with Diego. They were of a style worn at the beginning of the century and were particularly identified with the *soldaderas* who had fought alongside their men in the Mexican Revolution. She liked wearing them when with Diego, although she knew he was unaware of the symbolism that motivated her. Señora Mayet gently glided them onto her delicate feet.

Señora Mayet held for her the large, velvet-lined wooden box from which she carefully selected her jewelry: long gold chains lacing her elegant neck with gold coins; a heavy, pre-Columbian jade necklace; several gold rings on each hand; and innumerable gold bangle bracelets on both wrists. With the exception of her earrings, Diego had gifted all to her over the years.

Bedecked in her bright and colorful indigenous costume she looked – and felt – less frail. Not only did it help hide her polio-withered leg and numerous scars; it buoyed her withered spirit and emotional scars. She sat quietly by the window to await his arrival.

From her wheel chair she gazed beyond the gently billowing curtains across the far distance. Her mother, dead since 1932, was somberly observing her while holding in her arms Frida's three unborn children: wee, unformed fetuses destined to abort in pools of blood, tears, and nips of her heart. It was not the first time she saw her miscarried babies, but the image today consoled rather than disturbed her. "I'll be with you soon," she spoke aloud.

Her nurse opened the door and stuck her head in the room, "Did you call, Señorita?"

Frida, startled, suddenly laughed gaily. "No, no, Señora. I'm just visiting with my guests." Accustomed to her patient's eccentricities, Señora Mayet clucked her tongue and withdrew, closing the door quietly behind her.

Upon the death of her mother, Frida missed her deeply. Over the years, however, she was able to establish a direct two-way communication through which they comforted each other. Knowing that her aborted babies were lovingly attended by their grandmother eased the heartache of not being able to bear them into life – at least not into this life. Her shattered spinal column, pelvis, and internal organs allowed for them to be conceived but not born to this side of the veil.

"Oh, Mother. I'm so glad you're here." Frida spoke softly but animatedly while her mother continued to caress the babies. "Promise you'll stay by me when he comes?"

"For heaven's sake, Frida," her mother smiled. "You know we're always here."

"How do I look?" Frida adjusted the headdress and coquettishly lifted her long skirt above her ankles to show off her boots. "He never could resist my Tehuana aura." She threw back her head and shook with her loud, almost raucous laughter.

"Don't you think you should rest a bit until he arrives?" Her mother spoke disapprovingly but a soft smile tickled her lips. "And who knows when that will be; he's never come when expected in his life. I wouldn't be surprised if his mother had to carry him 10 or 11 months before he finally showed up for his own birth."

Frida laughed. "But isn't his arrival always worth the wait? You know you're as charmed by him almost as much as am I." Her smile disappeared as she quietly added, with an unaccustomed bitterness tinged with sadness, "As is too, evidently, my baby sister."

"That's over, Darling. You've forgiven her, and it's now time to forgive him."

Before she heard him, she felt the floor's vibration as he lumbered up the stairs. "Oh, Señor Rivera," she heard Señora Mayet greet him. "How good to see you. She's up and awaiting your arrival." Of all Frida's visitors, it was with only Diego did Frida detect the welcoming gaiety she now overheard.

Diego, flirtatious with most womyn and particularly so with womyn from whom he received such blatant adulation, tweaked her plump brown cheek. "Ah, but Señora, she is no longer my wife these many months past. I'm now free to run away with you." He affected a deeply serious tone, but his eyes flashed with the teasing spirit of their long running repartee.

"I'll run straight away to pack my bags," she threw over her shoulder – along with a girlish giggle – as she slipped into Frida's room to announce his arrival.

Frida was adjusting her headdress; her eyes sparkling with that bright luster only his presence engendered. The high excitement in Señora Mayet's voice as she bustled about the room – smoothing the bed, closing the armoire doors, and arranging Frida's long skirt to its best advantage – brought a sad smile to Frida's lips. She knew how much Señora Mayet loved Diego and how much their divorce had saddened her.

"Señorita, Señorita. He's here. Señor Rivera is here." Her voice was agitated with passion as she looked almost pleadingly upon her patient. "Oh, Señorita, he loves you so much. He loves none of the others the way he loves you."

Frida gently touched Señora Mayet's cheek and with a slight movement of her hand at once dismissed her and signaled to admit Diego.

He was elephantine and ugly, which accentuated Frida's fragility and beauty. His behemothic girth diminished her room; his Antaean voice shredded the gently billowing lace curtain. But his touch: his touch was gentle, quiet, almost feminine. His kiss on her cheek was but a whisper. "My Niña Fridita. How beautiful you look. How beautiful you are." Still panting heavily from his trudge up the stairs, he collapsed into the oversized chair built especially for him over 15 years ago. "How I've missed you."

All the heartache of the past ten months vanished as she saw his obscenely large, sensuous lips smile and his eyes exude the love she never doubted. For several moments they sat quietly gazing at each other. Theirs was the comfortable, trusting silence born of years of mutual knowledge; mutual love; mutual acceptance.

"You bastard. You ugly-toad bastard." Her whisper expelled from him any remaining doubts that she was ready, at last, to re-marry him.

"Yes." He slowly nodded his head, his rueful smile, boyish and puerile, lit his eyes with a sensuous wonder that evidenced the magic charm his unlovely beauty cast. "Yes, you know I am. I can't help it, but it doesn't mean I don't love you more than any thing or any other."

His letters of the past several months – none of which she answered – begged her to re-marry. His appeals were reasonable and each further healed the horrible hurt of his last affair. *I know you are hurting as much as I. Not more, my love, my Niña Fridita, my Life – not more, for yours is the hurt of the victim while I must bear the hurt of the offender. Your poor Ugly-Toad must bear the pain of having hurt his beloved, Child of My Soul, Child of My Eyes, Life of My Life, my own Chicuita. You have forgiven your sister, why won't you forgive me, your own Ugly-Toad who loves you as no sister could, as no mother, father, or god could love his Delicate Flower?*

She looked across the room at her dolls – the babies she was unable to bring to life. Yes, they needed their father. She needed their father. There was no life in their glass eyes or her black eyes in his absence. On the shelf beside her *niños* was the fetus in a glass jar of formaldehyde given to her by her dear friend – her doctorcito – Dr. Eloesser following her last spontaneous abortion. She had carried it home with her from San Francisco and found comfort in the tiny, curled body that – like her dolls and her many other miscarried babies – was denied life. Her loving care gave them life in this room, and their life nourished hers.

"There are conditions." Her voice, although no longer a whisper, remained in the sotto voce range that, none-the-less, revealed her somber and deep sadness.

"I would expect nothing else," he smiled. "You are my maestro."

"I will provide for myself financially from the proceeds of my own work. I will pay half of our household expenses – nothing more. And we will have no sexual intercourse."

"Oh, my Wee One. My Little Chicadee. I am so happy to have you back you could ask me to walk on burning coals each morning before breakfast, and I would assent." He heaved his massive bulk from the chair and danced comically before her.

Throwing her head back, with one hand steadying the head-dress, she laughed with the joy of the old days. Glancing at her dolls, she saw the light return to their glass eyes.

"We'll marry on my fifty-fourth birthday – December 8th. And now, my beautiful bride, I must return to work. My paintings thank you, my heart thanks you, and you will thank me." He kissed her hurriedly on the cheek and was gone.

"Señora Mayet." The door opened immediately and the broad smile on her glowing brown face spoke of her knowledge and her joy. "Oh, Señorita, now we will all be happy again." She busied herself removing the headdress and helping Frida back into bed. "Rest, now, Señorita. And dream happy dreams."

"No rest, Señora Mayet. Bring me my paints. How can I rest when I'm being re-born?" She glowed with happiness while her eyes searched for the life she knew she would find in the jarred fetus. "I will paint my birth before I die."

Beth

She could not recall when last she weighed herself. Was it two years ago next month? She was sure it was on an Easter morning, but of which one she was uncertain. Yes, she thought, it was 1998.

Easter was late this year: April 23rd. The first one of the twenty-first century. Maybe this century would be luckier for her than was the last.

She thought of Easter as the real New Year. How could anyone think of new beginnings in the depressive bleakness of a Massachusetts January? One was, she thought, far more likely to think of endings: death. Easter, on the other hand – yes – Easter was for new beginnings. Easter was the season of rebirth. The resurrection of Hope. The end of Winter's death.

Although not able to precisely pinpoint the year she last risked slowly lowering her bulk onto the scale, she recalled exactly the results. In preparation for the sacrifice of esteem, she took off all her clothes and sat on the toilet to urinate. She wondered how much her excretions weighed. Surely something.

She had placed the scale in the doorway of her closet. With her arms braced against each door jam, she could control the balance of her weight between the door frame and the scale. Gently and slowly – ever so slowly – she lowered her bulk until her arms hung loosely at her side.

Without looking toward her feet she stood perfectly still. She felt her throat constrict and tears well in her eyes. They silently coursed down each side of her nose, unable to negotiate the mass of her cheeks.

It may have been five minutes or five hours she stood quietly considering stepping off without reading the numbers. What difference did it make, she asked herself. She was fat and that was that. How fat didn't really matter, did it?

Her feet began to ache, but she resisted the urge to shift her weight, so as to prevent the scale from moving. With both hands she pressed in her bulging stomach, leaned slightly forward, and gazed down.

It took her a few moments to calculate what the numbers revealed. The red line quivered between 58 and 60. What could that mean? If only it meant she weighed one hundred and fifty eight. She knew that was impossible. She knew the truth. This was the third visit the red line had made to 58 since she began releasing her mass onto the brutally honest bathroom devil.

Two hundred and fifty eight pounds. Two hundred and fifty eight units of misery. Two hundred and fifty eight measures of shame.

The tears had stopped. She numbly picked up the scale and returned it to its corner in the bathroom. She walked to the kitchen, poured herself a glass of ice cold milk, unwrapped a pound of cheese, and took the box of Oreo's down from the cupboard where she had hidden them behind the dog food.

That was two years and many additional pounds ago. She knew she was fatter than ever – and shorter. She had always been five-four, but she felt she had shrunk. Maybe the gravity of her weight pressed her down toward the earth. Soon, she thought, if I am lucky, that same gravity will press me into the earth – into a grave – or into a gravity free future.

She had no sisters – of her blood or of her heart. She wondered how her life might have been different if she grew up with three sisters instead of three brothers. Her mother – dead these past ten years – was fond of pointing out that one daughter was more trouble than three sons put together. She never knew what that meant. She didn't see herself as any trouble. She didn't go anywhere, or get into trouble, or even argue with her brothers when they teased her about being fat and shy. She did okay in school and worked at the local bakery as soon as she turned sixteen. How was she any trouble? She must have asked herself that question thousands of times. She wished she had been able to ask her mother to explain it to her, but she was never able to ask her mother anything without being mocked. "Oh, Beth, honestly! What a question to ask." That's what her mother would have said, so what was the sense in asking?

At eighteen Him-Self asked her to run away with him to get married. She didn't even consider asking her mother; she just went. It was a sad little ceremony sans family, friends, or love. The Justice of the Peace and his wife were jaded, distracted, and rushed. She wondered what their wedding had been like. It was obvious what their marriage was like.

She thought of her husband as Him-Self, as, she was sure, he thought of himself. She never said the word out loud, but neither did she use his given name. She read somewhere that Hindu womyn never referred to their husbands by name out of respect and deference to their superiority. She didn't think it was respect that prevented her from using his name; it was more like he was not a real entity in her life. It would be sort of like giving a name to a lamppost. Sure, it gave you light and maybe even supported you when you were dizzy, but it didn't deserve a name.

It used to make her sad when the family, with much hilarity, told the story of the time she was in the hospital having his first baby and, when Him-Self was registering her, he could not remember which was her first name and which her middle name. To this day, the birth certificate of his oldest child has her first and middle name reversed.

As his babies came she gave them names but couldn't quite give them intimacy. She tried to think what her mother had done in her job of mothering, but all she could recall was her being there. Nothing much else. She laughed a lot with the boys and yelled a lot at her, but other than that she couldn't conjure a job-description for a mother.

The first two were boys and when his daughter was born she thought maybe she would keep her company. Maybe she could even be her friend when she got older. The first time his daughter rolled her eyes and said, "Oh, Mother, honestly! What a thing to say," she gave up on the idea of any friendship. His daughter was married now. So were his four sons. She rarely saw them, and when she did, she tried too hard to find things to talk about. They talked with Him-Self, and Him-Self talked with them, and she, for all her mass, remained invisible.

Him-Self claimed to have been raised a Quaker, yet he never attended any society meetings and sure didn't act like he revered any deity but Him-Self. Early in their marriage he mocked her when she went to the church she attended as a child. She liked going to church. It was pretty and peaceful. She never much listened to what the priest said, but she liked the singing. Even though she stopped going to church within a month or so of her marriage, she still thought of it with a melancholy yearning.

If Him-Self was a Quaker, she thought, than I'm a Quakee. It wasn't that she was actually afraid of him, but she certainly did quake at the thought of displeasing him. She had witnessed – or, rather, heard – his wrath when the boys were young. He would take them into the basement and beat them. She never saw it, but even when she covered her head with pillows and pressed her hands over her ears, she could hear the boys screaming and Him-Self's cold and measured counting of the blows.

He disciplined his daughter in a more calculated way and, strangely, it disturbed her more than the beatings he gave his boys. He simply refused to look at her or talk to her. He would announce at the supper table that he was *disappointed* in her behavior and that not only he, but her brothers and mother as well, would not look at her nor talk to her for a given period of time. Once the shunning lasted for over a month, but usually it went on for only a week or so. She almost wished he would beat her and get it over with.

And now she was alone. The five kids grown and gone. Him-Self was gone much of the time, also. He worked and golfed and ran. He called it jogging, but she called it running. She knew what he was running from, and she knew that, if she only had the courage, she would run from it too.

Instead, she spent her days on the old brown sofa eating cheese and watching soaps and game shows. Cheese was her only friend. She comforted her and filled the empty feeling inside. She kept her company and was always there when she needed her. She may not have sisters, but she had cheese. And, of course, Oreos.

And here it was almost Easter again. The kids would come to dinner with their families – well, all of them but the boy who ran away seven years ago, and they haven't heard of or from him since. She would serve the same meal she's served every year since the beginning. Did the early Christians – converted Jews – serve ham on Easter? Well, never mind, if she didn't serve ham, Him-Self would be *disappointed* in her, and her surprise announcement would be ruined.

His daughter helped her clear away the dishes while Him-Self and the boys talked football waiting for coffee and dessert to be brought. Their wives, chummy with one another but with neither her nor his daughter, chatted about their babies, their plastic surgeries, and their plans for the summer.

She sliced the coconut cake at the table and, as she passed each plate she wondered at her feelings of calm. The last serving passed, she said – not realizing it was almost a whisper – "Excuse me." The chatter continued, and she cleared her throat and repeated almost forcefully, "Excuse me."

As if in slow motion, each member of his family turned to look at her. Some had cake in their mouths, and they stopped chewing, while others paused with forks or coffee cups half way to their lips.

"Excuse me," she repeated calmly. "Tonight I'm going away." She paused, awaiting a reaction – a response – none came. They kept staring and slowly – ever so slowly – resumed chewing or lifting their forks or cups to their lips. It seemed a long time before Him-Self lowered his cup noisily onto the saucer. Before he could speak, she continued. "I've signed up for a womyn's retreat that was talked about on Oprah. I don't know when I'll be back." She turned from the table and with a soft "excuse me," went into the bathroom.

Satan was there in the corner where she had left him two years ago. She gazed at him, and slowly a smile began to form on her lips. She felt the rumble of laughter being born in her stomach and wending its way up, up, up until it burst vortex-like from her mouth.

She had packed her valise earlier and when she dragged it out from under the bed she opened it, took out the several blocks of cheese she had carefully tucked inside, and left them on his pillow.

They were still at the table when she carried her valise to the door. No one said a word as she smiled sweetly and said, "Goodbye."

The Old Womyn

The weary leaning barn meant little to anyone but the old womyn. One of the kids –wee Tommy – he loved her silly rambling stories – said she once told him the barn was born the same day as she.

That may or may not be true. Such sentimental trash always moved Tommy – he was rather a wimp. The only kid in the bunch with no interest in football.

The day they came to tear it down – which wasn't much of a job – it was ready to go with the next gust of wind anyway – Tommy leveled a stony stare and reminded them of their promise to wait . . . 'til after . . . .

The old womyn, they laughed, was blind as a bat and practically deaf to boot. Even if she could get out of her bed, she wouldn't see the shiny catalogue-bought shed in the barn's stead. Tommy always was rather a wimp – imagine thinking the old womyn would know . . . or care.

She was alone when she died late that afternoon. They told Tommy, and he asked, "Is the barn down?" They weren't sure if his silent tears were for the barn or the old womyn. He always was rather a wimp.

Faith

She knew – she had always known – her essence, her being, her *character* – was the result of more than that mingling of her parents' genes and her experiences. As a child she knew. As a teen she knew. As a young womyn she knew. And now, as she felt herself cross over into early old age, she *knew*.

~~ : ~~

On her sixth birthday Daddy left her: in a flurry of hysterical womyn, quietly sobbing men, and bewildered children; he simply was suddenly and mysteriously no longer there. Mother drew her aside from aunts, uncles, and cousins to gently and lovingly explain to her that Daddy had been absorbed into the Universe and would not return in the flesh. "It doesn't mean you don't have Daddy any more, my darling; only that no one but you will be able to see him."

"Will I be able to talk to him? Will he sing to me? Will he see the castles I build in the sand?"

"Yes."

Marked as the only fatherless child in her small New England village, she *knew* that distinction alone was not what made her different from the others. It was her awareness, perhaps from her long conversations with Daddy, that she had already chosen her destiny, her fate, her character. Regardless of her genes. Regardless of her environment. Her *chosen soul* was what her life would be.

~~ : ~~

High School: that time of pain and joy and self-centered doubt. For some – according to statistics (whatever they are!) for most – the outer limits of intellectual growth:

> American mass media is geared toward the level of a thirteen-year-old with the knowledge that some – according to statistics, most – Americans do not develop their vocabulary, reading level, comprehension, attention span, or intellectual curiosity beyond that with which they entered high school.
>
> – The Auburn Crier

Of others she was not sure, but of herself she was unequivocally certain: she had chosen her character, and she could and would continue to choose the developmental path it would take throughout her life.

When introduced to the concept of "Nature versus Nurture" and the denouement – thought to be so clever by her Introduction to Psychology teacher – of a delicate and customized dance of individually unique balance between the two, she was certain of the incompleteness of the formula.

"But, Mr. Carter, that's so, so – I don't know – depressing or something."

"Look, Faith, what else is there? We are only what we are: genetics and environment."

"Does that mean I can't do anything to direct my own life just because I'm stuck with my genes and whatever happened to me when I was a kid?"

She could hear the familiar groans of her classmates. Her questions – her arguments – her need to *know* somehow annoyed them.

"Well, I just can't buy that. It doesn't make sense. Why not just throw in the towel now if we have no input into what we are or can be? It makes life sound so, so . . . *boring.* So meaningless." She was straining forward in her seat, arms across the attached desk, her hands gripping the edges of the scarred and ugly wood. The intensity of her eyes desperate to engage this worn and weary teacher in her argument.

Classmates were collecting their books and quietly talking in anticipation of the bell that was about to release them to the throngs of noisy traffic in the corridor. From the dismissive smile on Mr. Carter's face and the escalating noise around her, she knew her skepticism of the accepted dogma was – yet again – viewed with barely disguised smirks and shaking of the heads. *"God, where does she come up with that stuff?"*

"Okay, people, Chapter Seven for Monday. Be prepared for a quiz." He yelled over the cacophony of scraping chairs and jabbering students as they made for the door before the first notes of the jarring signal sounded. Mr. Carter was nothing if not determined to get through the textbook before the end of the semester.

~~ : ~~

A widow at thirty-two with three kids (not counting her *child within!)* {Sic!}, she accepted the re-absorption of her beloved husband into the same benign Universe that embraced Daddy. Her oldest, six-year-old Destiny, and the twins, four-year-old Hope and Charity; all so different one from the other and each working out the choreography of their unique individual dance of delicate balance between their shared genes, similar environment, and . . .

what? What was the other elusive ingredient in that formula – that secret recipe – for creating one's character?

> *When all the souls had chosen their lives, they went before Lachesis. And she sent with each, as the guardian of his life and the fulfiller of his choice, the daemon that he had chosen."*
> – Plato, *Republic,* Book X

What the Greeks referred to as *daemon,* the Romans called "genius," and Christians and Jews called "Guardian Angel." Faith had settled on the comfortable term, "soul."

It was her daemon, Genius, Guardian Angel, – her *Soul* – combined with her genes and experiences that determined the character she had *chosen.* And it was the individual souls of her three urchins that would allow them to similarly *choose* what they did with their genes and experiences. No genetic victim, she. No environmental victims, they. With awareness of *Soul* they could – would – custom design their own destiny with only an objective and passing nod to the *traumas* of childhood. Without an awareness of *Soul,* she knew they would be captives of their past. Her task was to allow them to become comfortably acquainted with their innate motivations – their unique souls that they alone would recognize.

~~ : ~~

Fifty-two. She continued to await her annunciation – that recognition of her own soul. The girls were now grown: beautiful in their Hope, Charity, and Destiny. Now her Faith must reveal itself in following her soul for the next thirty years or so. By eighty-two she hoped she would be gazing back over the years between now and then with a fondness for her realized and actualized soul; her motivational angel that was hers and hers alone.

The cusps of old age. She found it mysterious, frightening, exciting, and – above all – freeing. *Freeing.* The word sounded so contrived. So trite. So overused. Yet that was the sensation. She felt the freedom in her core. She could taste it in the air around her. She could embrace it like a child and rock it gently in her arms. She could clearly see – yes, *see* – her freedom: a warm candle glow that softened her features, diminished her intensity, and slowed her hurry. (Was it the alchemists that said, "All haste comes from the devil?") The freedom of her new stage (for surely the 50's are only a passing stage!) left her light and giddy, as after a haircut or a delicious flirtation.

She thought of Edna St. Vincent Millet's words: what were they? Ah, yes:

> *My candle burns at both ends,*
> *It shall not last the night.*
> *But ah, my foes, and oh my friends,*
> *It gives a lovely light*

And when she came across Alice Walker's ending poem in her novel *By the Light of My Father's Smile*, she, too, smiled in the light of her brightly burning candle:

> *When Life descends into the pit*
> *I must become my own candle*
> *Willingly burning myself*
> *to light up the darkness around me.*

Her character, her soul, her spirit – that which fueled her luminous candle – slowly emerged. Perhaps illuminated by her candle that only now – three-quarters through her life – became a cognitive part of her being. The annunciation – the revelation of the nature of her innate soul – could have come in any number of ways: a dream, a personal confrontation, a clearing of the psyche, a sagacious psychic or spiritual guide, a physical trauma, a moving aesthetic encounter. Annunciations, for those fortunate enough to be open to them, are unique to the individual. For her it was what suited her best: communion with Daddy, the first since she departed her childhood and entered those of her children.

~~ : ~~

"Okay, I'm over half way through my productive life, and I still don't know what I want to – (should?) – be doing with the next thirty years." She was sitting with Judith, her best friend, in their favorite Indian restaurant. "While the girls were young and needed me on a day-to-day basis, it was easy to recognize my role. But what now? Everyone I know seems to have found their niche in life: where and what best serves them and their search for meaning."

"Good grief, Girl. If anyone I know has a meaningful life, it's you. You're close to the kids and the grandkids. You have oodles of friends and activities. Your volunteer work at the shelter is valuable. What else are you looking for? You don't need to worry about money. What's missing?"

"I don't know. I can't put my finger on it but I figure I have a good twenty-five or thirty years left to really make a difference in my own life and maybe in the lives of others."

"You don't think raising three great kids makes a difference?"

Tears gathered at the corners of Faith's eyes. "Oh, I do. But that took so little time. Or the time it took went so quickly. Now what? Even when I was raising them – and loving every minute of it – I felt like there was a seed stirring inside me that was just waiting to be nurtured into something great. I still feel that stirring – it's, it's . . . " she groped for words, "it's damn unsettling. And here I am heading toward sixty, and I haven't yet figured out what the nature of that seed is. What it would grow into if only it was fed and watered."

Judith moved her water glass to the side as she reached across the table to take Faith's hands. She silently held them for a minute giving them a tender squeeze before releasing them. Faith appreciated her silence and refrain from offering superficial, banal assurances. Until now she had not vocalized her feelings to Judith – or anyone else for that matter – and was frankly confused by her passion and calenture.

"It's not that I don't love my life. I do. It's just that – I don't know – it probably sounds egocentric – but it's just that I know – I *know* – I should be doing something . . . something more. Or something else. Or something meaningful. And it feels like this is the time."

"'Should'?" Judith laughed. "'Should'? Hey, aren't you the one who preaches that we must not 'should' on ourselves or allow anyone else to 'should' on us?"

It was raining when they hugged goodbye in the parking lot. "Give the kids my love." "See you Tuesday at the book group." "Drive carefully." "Love ya." "Love ya."

~~ : ~~

The ride home was slow. The torrential desert rain made her night driving more difficult than usual and her musings turn to her love of the desert. No rain is more passionate than desert rain. Perhaps the long droughts between draughts increase the urgency of our thirst and the intimacy of our satiation. Of all Nature's copulations, that between desert and sky is the most ardent, ferocious, and savage – sex in its feral state. Her love of the desert was deep and abiding, matching – and in part forming – her own nature. The rain never failed to bring her to wonder at the relationship between an individual's character – her soul – and her geography. *Yes, more than anyplace, I am desert.*

No sooner did the thought enter her consciousness than did her father. It was not a *memory* of Daddy – it *was* Daddy. As with a dear friend, it was as though the years between visits were erased, and the last conversation was simply continued and casual. "Did you discover your soul before you died, Daddy? You were so young when you passed over."

"Age is irrelevant, Bunny Cheeks. My annunciation came when I was a kid. I always, *always* knew I would play the violin and that my playing would be my soul. My character. The Guardian Angel of my time on Earth. Before I was even able to hold a full-sized fiddle I was aware it was my destiny."

"But how did you know? What did it feel like? What were the signs that you were experiencing your soul's annunciation?" She heard her voice take on the tone of her childhood when she was Bunny Cheeks to the family. After Daddy's passing, the nickname was never again used.

"You're right. There are signs all around. For you, since you have been around longer, there are more signs than most."

"Thanks for reminding me how long I've been around." She laughed. She felt gay and delighted with the visitation. "Daddy, I don't even know where to start looking."

"Remember when Francis stole your body shortly after I died? You successfully retrieved it and never again allowed anyone to possess it against your will. Well, so much of your life has been connected to that rapine. For you, the trauma was resolved early on, and you thought it was no longer part of you. But look around you: you had three girls that you were able to raise to healthy womynhood; without your urgent encouragement your two friends, Tish and later, Estelle, would not have sought psychotherapy for their rape trauma (never mind that Estelle's first therapist made the word into two!); you're drawn to womyn's literature; you surround yourself with womyn friends; you're an active feminist; you chose to volunteer at a womyn's shelter. If these aren't signs in your life, what are?"

She rarely, if ever these days, thought of her childhood sexual abuse. Her innate strength, self-confidence, and self-determination – and her long, therapeutic talks with Daddy at the time – diminished its negative effect. In fact, she often wondered if the abuse had served to reinforce and intensify her love of the feminine and womynhood and her determination to direct her own life: to find her soul. "Daddy," she asked teasingly, "Are you the Angel Gabriel? Is this my annunciation?"

"Well, Bunny Cheeks, if it looks like a duck, and quacks like a duck . . . ." His smile lit up the car; he radiated love and intelligence. "Maybe you've found the nature of your seed and now just have to find your way of nurturing it."

"Will you be my co-nurturer? Will you visit more often?"

"I've been around all along; you just weren't ready to resume our talks."

~~ : ~~

The opening of Desert Rain Crisis Center (DRCC) was scheduled for the Saturday after Thanksgiving. Destiny came into town early to help with the preparations. Hope and Charity would arrive with the kids on Wednesday and stay through Sunday. Faith could not recall when she was more excited – ebullient. She had always loved Thanksgiving as the start of the holiday season. This Thanksgiving would be the start of the holiest season of her life – the final twenty or thirty years. The advent of her soul. At last – long last – her character had emerged, and the incredible lightness of her being was palpable to those around her.

Thursday was filled with fun, kids, food, friends, and all the wonderful festivities of the uniquely American observance. Her small apartment seemed capable of feeding the world and embracing the Universe. She had chosen this time of year for the opening when, over a year ago, she arranged for the sale of her home to make DRCC possible. She couldn't believe (so to speak, as she certainly had belief all along!) that it was finally going to happen. DRCC would begin seeing patients – men, womyn, and children – on Monday morning. Not many, as its capacity was limited, but the few it would serve over the coming years would be served with love, compassion, and intelligence. They would emerge with a greater understanding of soul, character, and destiny. They would emerge whole. They would be prepared for their own enunciations.

She was physically tired, financially broke, and never happier in her life. Her soul rejoiced.

Saturday dawned bright, warm, and sunny. Setting up the borrowed folding chairs on the lawn outside the small rented office left her overheated and sticky. The cookies and punch (no black-tie gala this!) were on tables under the Palo Verde. The guests began arriving slowly, and the clouds gathered rapidly. By 2:00 the decision was made to squeeze chairs, punch, cookies, and guests inside. Now everyone was overheated and sticky, none-the-less all had caught Faith's contagious ebullience. The rains came down and refreshed their souls. The drought was past. The desert rejuvenated.

Rosalind

She felt the high desert in her soul: the vastness, the solitude, the stark beauty of infinite possibilities. Nowhere had she felt closer to the sky; the terror of her searing sun, the closeness of her diamondesque stars. She understood why so many seekers of wisdom throughout the ages retreated to the desert for enlightenment. Nowhere else had she so deeply experienced Nature as her partner in creation: her terrible Muse.

Oceans, forests, mountains, and lakes were distant cousins to the desert: poor relations flaunting their jewels in a futile attempt to outshine their quietly self-confident cousin. The desert would be her home: the place for which she would yearn when life took her afar. The place where her soul found solace, serenity, and succor.

Little more than a shack, the cabin was neither insulated nor air-conditioned. Fifty miles north of Phoenix, it sat on the south side of a mountain in the Tonto National Forest overlooking the lower desert as it stretched south and west toward the distant city in the valley below. The nearest town was ten miles as the crow flies and twice that as her geriatric Toyota pick-up wended its way every four to six weeks over rutted dirt trails down the mountain for supplies.

Owned by the National Park Service and leased for $100.00 a year, the cabin was one room – 15 feet by 18 feet – with an attached shed and pump room. In the far corner of the north wall were a toilet and a cot that she had partitioned from the room with shoulder-high bookshelves perpendicular to the wall. The south wall was punctuated in the center by the only door, which was flanked by a small window on each side.

Under the window to the right of the door was a rustic sink set in a rough-hewn counter with a clean white skirt tacked to the rim to enclose utensils and cleaning products stored beneath. On the counter beside the sink was a clean white Rubbermaid mat with a lip that curved into the sink. On the mat was a matching dish drain in which she stored a large, clear, heavy plastic drinking glass, a manual can opener, a cork screw, three wooden spoons of various sizes, a rubber spatula, and an assortment of kitchen knives covered by a clean, white dishtowel.

By the counter was a sturdy metal utility table supporting an electric, two-burner cooking unit and a new white

Hitachi bread machine with a rice making feature. On the floor under the table was a large white Rubbermaid ice chest in which she stored her non-perishable food: cereals, crackers, rice, powdered milk, pasta, dry cat food and canned goods: tuna, soups, vegetables, fruits, Boston baked beans, brown bread.

Wedged between the utility table and the west wall gleamed – incongruously large – a new white side-by-side Amana. The appliance store had charged an exorbitant delivery fee, but it was well worth having a refrigerator large enough to store ample perishables to last for several weeks.

In front of the window to the left of the door was a large, oblong table with two chairs. One chair was neatly tucked into the far end of the table, and the other was positioned at the center of the table facing the window. The table and chairs, like the sink counter, appeared to be hand-made of the same rough-hewn, dark wood. The table served as both her dining area and desk. While ninety percent of the table was covered with books, magazines, journals, newspaper clippings, papers, pencils and pens, overflowing file trays, stationary, and plastic containers for paper clips, rubber bands, stapler and staples, staple remover, scissors, scotch tape, post cards, mailing tape, and stamps, it was the small uncluttered portion at the far end that drew one's attention.

Separated from the working portion of the table by a long, low, Waterford crystal bowl set off on each side by white candles in sparkling silver candle sticks was her small dining area. Permanently set for one, a narrow, white linen table runner ran across the width of the table, gracefully falling on each side to the floor. A dinner plate, salad plate, and cup and saucer of the finest English bone china were carefully arranged. The pattern was ornate: Aynsley Imperial with a broad boarder of black and gold. Sterling silver forks, spoons, and a knife flanked the dinner plate. The Irish linen napkin matched the table-runner and was artfully folded in the semblance of a swan and placed on the dinner plate. A Waterford crystal Lismore water goblet and wineglass completed the table setting.

The remaining three walls were floor to ceiling bookcases she had built herself from lumber and cinder blocks laboriously carted up the mountain in her ancient truck.

They were the resting-places for her closest friends: books that had accompanied her through her tumultuous childhood, books she cherished from her college days, and books she had invited into her life since.

Her front yard was hundreds of acres of mesquite, palo verde, and iron wood trees watched over by thousands of statuesque saguaros. Her high desert forest was no less nurturing to the spirit than the forest of Arden, to which her namesake had retreated.

She sat outside the front door dreamily absorbing the scarlet, fuchsia, and lavender sky that had kissed the sun goodnight only moments before. It was just after 7:30 and the scorching 106-degree heat of the day was being swept away by a light breeze that frequently visited at that hour. Wave after wave of mountains receded ever more faintly toward the west and east, until those farthest melted into mist unsure if they were mountains or imaginations. Soon the lights of the Valley of the Sun, at the heart of which reigned Phoenix, would begin to dot the view to the south. The combination of a clear night and a dreamy mood turned the city lights into a distant sea reflecting the desert stars and milky moon.

"Certainly, this is our favorite time of day," she murmured to Orlando who purred more loudly at the sound of her voice. The old cat, contentedly stretched out on her lap, nudged his forehead against her hand to remind her to continue scratching his neck. She laughed quietly and resumed her idle petting while abandoning herself to the sensuous desert sky.

She was neither asleep nor fully conscious. Hours or days might have passed before she roused herself, suddenly aware of a chill. Orlando felt her stir and raised his blue eyes in query. *Is it time for dinner?*

"Come on, Ol' Boy," she gently lifted him off her lap onto the ground where he stretched, yawned and wound his sinuous Siamese body between her ankles. "Time for din-din."

The house was still warm. She closed only the screen door and opened both windows inviting the cool desert night to enter through the screens. She turned on the soft lamp by her cot and pulled out a bin from under the cot from which she selected a white cotton shift. She took off her jeans and shirt, draped them over the metal rod at the foot of the cot and walked in her underpants to the kitchen sink where she filled the large water pitcher with cool water. She returned to her bedside table where she carefully poured the water into the matching basin and bathed herself with the white terry clothe that hung from the metal rod at the head of her cot. The lilac scented soap always reminded her of her mother and she never failed to smile at the memory. The terry face clothe rung dry and draped back on the metal rod, she gently dried herself with the matching terry bath towel. It was soft and also smelled of lilac from the scented fabric softener she added to the dryer at the laundromat in town. Refreshed, she slipped into her clean cotton dress.

Orlando sat patiently watching her ritual ablutions. He knew his dinner would follow this nightly routine. Dry food in the morning – enough to last through the day if he felt like an occasional nibble. The good stuff in the evening: he turned his aristocratic nose up at anything but Sheba. And it must be chicken, turkey, or duck: he refused the white fish or the beef.

While he dined leisurely on the evening viands, she prepared her one meal of the day. Her morning juice could not be considered a meal, and the gallon of water she drank during the day was all that sustained her until evening.

The small cabin was turned into a concert hall by the combination radio/CD tuned to KBAQ 89.5. The Bose speakers filled the small space with the exquisite magic of Debussy, Brahms, Mozart, Tchaikovsky, Schubert, Strauss, and Chopin.

She lit the candles on the table and sat down to curried chicken and rice, a fruit and yogurt salad, iced cranberry juice mixed with ginger ale, and ice water. Reviewing her day, she felt content: the problem that had vexed her in the fourth chapter of her book was resolved, and she was able to see the plot through to a satisfactory denouement. She felt confident she would be able to deliver this, her third novel, to her publisher by the date promised.

She ate slowly. Deliberately. Mindfully. The curry was hot and perfectly complemented by the cool yogurt and fruit salad. Indian cuisine was her favorite and always brought her back to her love of Indian culture: the music, certainly, but most particularly, the poetry. "Perhaps tonight I will forego finishing Annie Dillard's new novel and instead take down Rabindranath Tagore." Long forgotten lines came to her mind that she thought were Tagore's:

> *As the sun sets in the horizon,*
> *When masses of clouds look like flowers*
> *In the sky,*
> *I float away somewhere far off.*
> *And in my mind,*
> *I burst open the closed door,*
> *Of a fairy tale home.*

"Is mine a fairy tale home?" she wondered. Out loud she queried, "Orlando, is ours a fairy tale home? What do you think, huh?" By now finished with his dinner, he sat in the center of the room grooming his whiskers and preparing for the quiet evening ahead. At her voice he sent her a sweet mew and continued his toilette.

She cleared her dishes from the table and gently washed them in the sink. She dried them carefully and replaced them in their original place on the table ready for the next day's meal. She loved these plates and caressed them almost affectionately while she washed and dried them. They had been her mother's, and she often wondered with amusement what her mother would think if she saw them in this rustic mountain cabin. For that matter, what would she think of her daughter living alone with a cat in this isolated retreat in the high Sonoran desert?

She found her Tagore, and before sitting in the one easy chair in which she read, she wrapped her Pachima around her shoulders and closed the windows and door. The evening chill had found its way into the cabin and the heat of the day was banished.

As she switched on the floor lamp behind her chair, she noticed Orlando become alert and perk his ears in the direction of the door. In the two years she had lived here, she had never had any visitors; invited or uninvited. Unless she counted the numerous rattlesnakes, coyotes, mountain lions, Gila monsters, tarantulas, deer, and the wide variety of desert birds, she could honestly say she had never been disturbed in her retreat. None of the critters that wandered by were a disturbance: giving her as wide a berth as she gave them. All, that is, but the scorpions that occasionally found their way into the damp corners of the pump house. Now those critters were nasty.

"It's okay, Boy. It's probably a coyote hoping to find you on the other side of the door. Come on up and read." She pursed her lips with a kissing sound and patted her lap for Orlando to join her. "Come on, Boy." With a backward glance toward the door, he stretched, yawned, and gracefully leaped into her lap. She smiled as he performed his usual ritual of tight circles before settling down with one paw lightly resting on her arm.

Tagore seeped into her soul and lulled her into a peaceful sleep. She dreamed of three seas caressing each other in shades of aqua, and as she dreamed, she was aware she was dreaming and was delighted with the dream she had chosen.

Her halcyon pool of sleep slowly ebbed: without opening her eyes she was aware of a presence in the room. She smelled the sweet spicy Tweed of her childhood: her mother's favorite scent. How many Mothers' Days had she bought her Tweed dusting powder, cologne, or body lotion? Did they even make Tweed any more? She must find out when next she visited the city.

She was now fully conscious but continued to cling to the present by refusing to open her eyes. She knew that once she abandoned blindness, nothing would be the same.

Orlando nudged her hand. He, too, was aware of the presence and wanted her to join them. She gently moved her fingers to scratch behind his ears and, with a sigh of resignation, opened her eyes.

Mother was standing by the sink. "It's about time you decided to wake up, Sleepy Head." Her voice held the gentle mocking affection Rosalind would recognize anywhere. She was not in the octogenarian body in which she had died but the handsome 50-something body Rosalind remembered from her teen years. She looked strong and healthy and happy. "You don't seem surprised to see me."

"I knew you would come sometime, but I thought it would be a time when I was in trouble: unhappy or sick or something." Rosalind did not rise from the chair, yet she felt the embrace of her mother. She smiled. "You have no idea how I've missed you, Mother."

"You know I'm always with you, my angel girl. You just need to listen for my voice. I've been with you every step of the way since I passed in...was it '92 or '93? Time flies when you're having fun." Her laughter filled the small cabin and startled Orlando. He jumped down from Rosalind's lap, scurried under the table, and sat attentively observing. "Sometimes complacency is trouble, Darling. I'm here to shake you up a bit."

"Mum, I've never been happier. I'm reading, writing, and meditating and don't have a care in the world."

"That might just be the trouble. You don't have a care in the world because you've divorced the world. The cares of the world are still there; you've just decided to turn your back on them." Mother spoke matter-of-factly with a softness that balanced the directness of her words.

"You've got to be kidding. You're the one who always advocated the benefits of retreats. My spiritual quest has been enhanced by retreating to the desert, and I thought you, of all people, would approve."

"You've done fine, Darling. But remember the whole point of the spiritual quest is to more fully engage with and in life. The real test of your spiritual growth is how you interact with life, not how long you can retreat from it." Mother approached the chair and sat on the edge of the ottoman upon which Rosalind's feet rested. "The spiritual quest is the road toward helping ourselves live more fully and helping others do the same." She began massaging Rosalind's feet. "Do you still love foot massages?"

"Ahhh, that feels so good. No one gives massages like you." She stretched her legs so her mother would have better access to her feet. "It's so peaceful here, Mum. I hate the thought of returning to the turmoil and chaos of being with people."

"Maybe you can use the growth you've achieved over these two years to diminish that turmoil and chaos. Share it with others." Mother stood up and slowly gazed around the small cabin. "I have to leave now, My Baby Girl. I know you will follow the right path. You still have a long journey ahead, and the quest continues."

"Oh, Mother, do you have to go so soon? There's so much I want to tell you. So much I want to ask." Rosalind started to rise from her chair, but Mother smiled and motioned her to remain seated. She sank back into the chair. "Please stay."

"I'm with you whether or not you see me. Just listen for my voice." She began to turn then, with a second thought, turned back to Rosalind. "I love your dining room, Darling. This place is you– most definitely you. Come to think of it, it's me too." Her laughter again rang through the small cabin and she was gone.

For the first time in her two years in the high desert cabin, the silence felt austere, unhealthy, and unfulfilling. "Come on, Boy. Let's get into bed. Tomorrow we'll talk."

Mrs. Rousseau

She told her story with a raspy, flat blandness with a voice of thick oil leaking out of a rusty tin can. Her eyes, raised fleetingly to assure herself she was not alone or that I had not fled in horror, spoke more loudly than her words. "This is the first I've spoken of it in all these years." She paused, concentrated for a few moments on pushing back the quick of her left thumb with the nail of her right thumb, sighed quietly and continued. "Whatever happens, happens. I don't care any more. I just want . . . ." Her eyes fluttered up searching mine before hastily returning to her aged hands. "I just want someone to know the truth. It's time. There have been so many rumors over the years. So many . . . ." Her voice trailed off as she gazed out the window: she was no longer aware of my presence: while her frail body remained seated in the same straight-backed chair, she had drifted from the room.

Aunt Olive had died suddenly: my weekly visits to her over, Sunday afternoons yawned deliciously before me. I missed Olive. My mother's sister, she had been the oddest one in an odd family of three sisters and two brothers. The last of the O'Connor siblings, her death – peaceful in sleep – marked my graduation into the ranks of the older generation. It was a systemic shock to realize the probability that my nieces and nephews – and grand nieces and nephews – perceived my sisters and me as we had perceived our parents and their siblings: out of touch, sexless, settled, and ineffectual.

It had been over six weeks since Olive was buried when I was surprised to receive a message from the Sunrise Nursing Home: Maude Rousseau, Olive's roommate for the eleven years she resided there, had asked to see me.

I had intended to drive down to Portland to spend the weekend with friends, but due to my natural curiosity and inbred courtliness, Sunday morning found me headed Down East as had so many Sunday mornings over the past eleven years. After all, a gentleman did not stand up a lady, never mind that the lady in question was an octogenarian with a dark and ominous history.

Route 1 never ceased to charm: from Orono, my university surroundings fell behind as it occurred to me that I missed the weekly drive through the small towns and villages along the Bold Coast of Washington County. In Machias I stopped for my customary lunch at Helen's. As much as I enjoyed their famous blueberry pie – judged the best blueberry pie in blueberry country – I enjoyed the view from the dike of Machias River as it emptied into Machias Bay.

It was mid-August, but the low sixties temperature and gray, overcast sky misting persistently but almost imperceptibly imbued a sense of summer's end as I relished the last crumbs of my dessert. A fog lay low over the water obscuring the rugged ledges beyond. Despite the warmth of the restaurant, I felt a slight chill.

It had been my custom to bring a whole blueberry pie with me for Aunt Olive. She enjoyed parceling it out piece by piece to her favorite nurses, aides, and sister residents. As I considered whether to bring one for Mrs. Rousseau, I was aware how little I knew her. Although I greeted her cordially each time I visited Aunt Olive, I soon learned not to engage her in conversation, as the least bit of attention given elsewhere piqued Olive's jealousy.

During my weekly visits with Olive, I was always vaguely aware of Mrs. Rousseau's presence: ostensibly reading silently on her side of the institutional room, I suspected she was actually carefully following our conversations. Her harmless eavesdropping did not disturb me: quite the contrary, as it was evident those conversations were the only ones in which she could participate – if only vicariously – with someone from the outside world. In my years of visits to Olive, I had never seen her receive a visitor, letter, gift, or greeting card, nor had I ever heard her utter a sound beyond guttural grunts in response to queries from aides and nurses. If my family news and tidbits of this and that which I shared with Aunt Olive brought pleasure to her infamous roommate, I did not begrudge her.

"Are you ready for your check, Professor?" The waitress, a former student, had dropped out of school to marry her high school sweetheart. "Shall I wrap up a pie to go?"

"Thanks, Sally. You're looking well."

Tucking her hands under her belly, she pulled her blue uniform snug to show off her waistless figure. "Third one on the way," she grinned happily while tallying the check. "I'll getcha ya pie. Catch it on ya way out."

After leaving a healthy tip; not so much as to embarrass or insult her, I followed her to the cashier stand at the end of the counter. "Take care of those boys, and say 'hi' to Bud from me."

"Oh, I will, Professor. He's out fish'n with 'em now. We're hop'n this one's a girl so we can name ahh boat afta her – when we get a boat, that is." She laughed gaily. "Say 'hi' to ya aunt from me."

Before I could tell her of Olive's passing, she waved and bustled off toward the kitchen.

In East Machias I turned onto 191 and drove out to Quoddy Head. The mist had turned to heavy drizzle and the gray sky had darkened threateningly. I determined not to stay long so as to avoid driving back to Orono in the storm that appeared imminent.

Mrs. Rousseau sat by the window in her straight-backed chair. No one had yet been moved into Aunt Olive's side of the two-bed room: it was startling to see the starkness created by her absence. Devoid of Olive's profusion of family pictures, cards, knick-knacks, flowers, and other personal possessions, the lack of them on Mrs. Rousseau's side of the room was more noticeable.

Mrs. Rousseau looked up as I entered but neither smiled nor acknowledged my arrival. "Hello, Mrs. Rousseau. I've brought you a blueberry pie."

"Sit there." Her voice was cracked from lack of use – dry, phlemmy. Her lips didn't move as her raspy breath hissed between them. She pointed her trembling hand toward a chair across from her. I placed the pie on the bed and sat in the chair, a chair I had never seen anyone occupy in the past.

"You're looking well, Mrs. Rousseau." I had never really looked at her before. In the hundreds of times I had sat on the other side of the room, I had never taken notice of her physicality that was so unlike my aunt's. She was tall and wiry with wispy white hair that scarcely covered a bright red scalp. Her long face was ruddy and deeply creased as that of an ol' salt who had seen many seasons at the prow of a fishing vessel. Her chin was cavernously porous with a soft white beard that appeared never to have been plucked. Her nose was pure cartilage and sharp bone, sans flesh: if the day were sunny, it would cast a prominent shadow over her large, lipless mouth. The long white hairs beneath her nostrils moved with her breath, while one particularly long tendril curled into the dark recesses of her gaping gob. Presiding over this remarkable assortment of features were bulging, lidless eyes: huge yellow spheres with black, pupil-less irises having no evidence of either contraction or dilation. Through these eyes no soul could be witnessed.

"Please close the door." Incongruously, her voice was so soft as to be almost a whisper. I quietly closed the door and resumed my seat.

She had drifted from the room, and my discomfort was increasing. Should I break the silence to recall her to the present? "Mrs. Rousseau, why do you want to tell your story to me?" She did not, as I had feared, start at my intrusion into her silence. Rather, she turned back toward me and resumed where she had left off.

"I have spoken of it to no one. It's time rumors and speculation are put to rest. Who else would I tell? You are my only friend."

Unaware of the pathos of her words, she began: "You're young. As young as I was when it all happened. You don't know what it was like during those days. The war in Europe had just begun, or rather had just begun for us. Most of the boys and men in the village had shipped out and those who were left were the old or lame. I didn't live in Lubec then. I lived with my mother and aunts at Cutler Harbor. Have you been out to Cutler?"

Without expecting or awaiting a reply she continued. She had moved her attentions from the quick of her left thumb to that of her left index finger. Gently pushing back the delicate skin with her thumbnail she would then lovingly caress the finger between the soft pads of her right thumb and index finger.

"It's a beautiful village. I was born there and never lived anywhere else – nor wanted to. Our house was on Destiny Bay Road on the western side of the harbor. Daddy used to say we could live off the sea and the land better than any one in the world could live anywhere. I fished, clammed, and hauled lobster with the other children, and in the summers we ate so many wild blueberries, black berries, and raspberries Daddy used to say we had become feral."

She laughed quietly: she was talking neither to me nor to herself now but to some misty memory of her former self. Both speaker and listener were enjoying the conversation.

"When Daddy and the boys went off to fight the war, I just kept on fishing, clamming, and hauling with the few men who remained. I wanted Daddy to be proud of me when he returned." She paused for what seemed minutes. "He never came home."

My chair, an armless metal folding number intended for church suppers or card games, was hard, unfriendly. She did not notice me shift uncomfortably.

"When I married Him I thought he would be like Daddy: kind and fun and wise. Instead he was mean, humorless, and stupid. There is nothing more dangerous than a stupid person – man or womyn. He didn't want me to continue working. I think he feared being shown up. He knew I could handle a boat or a line better than most men could.

"When the babies started coming I thought I could suffer his vicious tongue and mean-spirited ways. He never drank. I can say that much for him. But, somehow, he was worse than a mean drunk was. He was cunning and conniving and seemed to plot and relish his viciousness.

"When I talked about him to Mother, she said at least he didn't hit me. I never dreamed he'd beat the boys, but he did, and for the most minor infractions. Kid's stuff. They were good boys, my boys. They never did anything bad. He'd take them down into the basement and beat them with a heavy oak paddle he made especially for that purpose. I would be in the kitchen, and would hear him talking coldly to them as they screamed in fear and pain. He prided himself on his method of beating them when he was not angry. "I just want to show them who's boss," he would say.

"After every beating they would come back upstairs, their eyes red, and I could see the shame and hatred in their demeanor. As they got older the beatings grew more frequent, and the shame and hatred grew more noticeable. There was no more screaming, though. It was as if the three boys decided they would deprive him of some of the pleasure he derived from the beatings. They would come back upstairs and their eyes were no longer red but steely and hard. They wouldn't look at me or at each other. Their shame and hatred was too raw.

"Ours was a silent and angry house. No one spoke but Him, and He searched for searing words to burn our spirits and weld our lips shut.

"Marcus, the middle boy, was only 12 when he first ran away. He kept finding him and dragging him home until, finally, when he was 17, He couldn't find him anymore. We never saw nor heard from him again. I don't know if he's alive or dead. What I do know though is his Daddy sure ain't alive." She chuckled.

"He broke his arm that winter, and without Marcus, I had to haul with the boys. It wouldn't have been bad if He had not insisted on coming even though he couldn't do anything but criticize.

"We were headed back toward the harbor and had the Little River light house in sight. It had been a good haul, and I felt some grim satisfaction in the day. I couldn't help thinking of how different it had been after a good day of hauling with Daddy. We would be excited and happily singing. I couldn't remember the last time I had seen my boys laugh and knew I had no laughter left in me.

"My oldest boy, Will, was at the helm. The water had gotten rough but nothing our boat couldn't handle. We were approaching the island when He yelled for him to speed up. 'You're poking like an ol' lady,' he hollered, 'We'll never get home at this rate.'

"I don't know what Will was thinking. He seemed to just snap. He violently shoved the throttle forward and the prow jumped out of the water as we sped forward. With His arm and all, He lost his balance and was thrown into the water."

She became silent as she gazed out over the Passamaquoddy Bay toward Eastport. The sky had darkened, and the drizzle had graduated to a full-fledged squall. I wanted to shift my weight in the chair but hesitated for fear of disturbing her. I don't know how long it was she remained silent: sitting ramrod straight staring through the window into the past. The lights of Eastport had come on before she continued.

"Will turned and saw Him go overboard at the same time my baby and I regained our balance and realized what had happened. He pulled back on the throttle and circled back toward Him. He was thrashing about in the water with his broken arm and all. I couldn't tell what he was yelling, but he sure was hollering something.

"None of us said a word. The boat drifted closer to Him, and still none of us moved. We just stood staring at him in the dark water. Will started the boat, and we headed for the harbor.

"The body was never found. At the inquest, they speculated the heavy cast on his arm pulled him down. The morning after the inquest both boys left Cutler, and I've neither seen nor heard from them since. That was fifty years ago. I've been in one nursing home or another ever since until I came here fifteen – or is it 18 – years ago. I guess this is where I'll die."

The room had become dark, and I rose to turn the overhead light on. I was at a loss for words, and it was evident she had no more to say. I glanced at my watch and was dismayed at the time.

There was a soft knock at the door, and an aide cautiously stuck in her head. "I'm sorry to interrupt, Mrs. Rousseau, but your dinner is ready. Do you want me to bring it in?" I was struck by the fact that she was called Mrs. Rousseau when Aunt Olive was always called by her first name.

Mrs. Rousseau made a soft grunt and nodded affirmative. I remembered she had not spoken to anyone since her arrival, and it was rumored she had not uttered a word since the "accident."

While the aide positioned her dinner tray on the bed table, I rose awkwardly. "I must leave now, but I will come and see you again if you would like." She had retreated into her silence – perhaps the silence of that boat long ago – and gave no sign of having heard me. "Goodbye, Mrs. Rousseau."

She was attending to her meal and was oblivious of her surroundings. I quietly departed and was headed for the lobby when an officious nurse approached. "Professor, it's good to see you again. I didn't expect you'd be back after your aunt's death. I want you to know we all miss her."

"That's very kind of you. Thank you."

It was obvious she had more to say, and I gave her no easy route to the inquiries I guessed she wanted to make. Seeing my intention to move on with no further conversation, she rapidly continued.

"We were all so surprised, and pleased – er, yes, pleased – so see you visiting Mrs. Rousseau. She never has visitors, you know."

"Yes, well, thank you again. And goodbye."

She was more forceful, now. "Uh, Professor. Mrs. Rousseau has not talked to anyone to my knowledge in many years. Did she talk to you? Did she have anything of import to say that I should know of?"

I smiled pleasantly. "No, Nurse, nothing of import of which you should be apprised. Good night."

I slept poorly that night with dreams of hands reaching for me through the fog. At seven the following morning, I received a call from the Sunrise Nursing Home with the news that Mrs. Rousseau had passed peacefully in her sleep.

Nora

I tell you there is such a thing as creative hate!
– Willa Sibert Cather *The Song of the Lark (1915)*

She knew she was a prime candidate for a heart attack, and that if she did not soon execute her long-thought-out plan for revenge, she may never have a chance to enjoy it. At 58, five feet one inch tall and 138 pounds, Nora lived life well – in itself a form of revenge but nowhere near the revenge she had in mind. Oh, no. Nowhere near what she had in mind.

Is it possible it was fifty years since she began developing what would eventually become her ultimate plan? Fifty years? No, it couldn't be. Surely it couldn't be that long. But, yes, it was. She was eight when he first began giving her that sicky-icky feeling, and here she was 58. Barbie, her daughter and best friend, was almost forty, and Ranger, her baby boy, was thirty-six. The wonder of their ages always startled her. Why, she didn't think of herself as much older than thirty – how could her children be older than she herself? My, she thought, before long my grandbabies will be as old as me. As it was, her first grandbaby was exactly the age she had been when it all first began. Eight. So young. So very innocent. So vulnerable to evil.

Yes, it's time to make it happen. To wreak the revenge on him that he so deserves.

Life had not been as good to him as it had been for her. And she would know. Not many folks wrote into their budgets an annual expense for a private investigator. Every year, year after year for the past thirty years, she received a succinct update on his whereabouts including his family and work circumstances. She was interested only in knowing where he was so that when the time came she would be able to wreak the revenge that had remained constant in her thoughts all these years.

Williams & Son
Licensed and Bonded
Private Investigators

Francis W. Robus
2001

Address –   4 Highland Terrace, Portland, Maine
Employer –   Robus Real Estate, Owner/Broker
Family –   Divorced (wife remarried)
                       4 children, 10 grandchildren:
                       Clarissa Connors – divorced,
                       three children: (Carl, Chris, Cassie),
                       lives with father;
                       Frank Robus, Jr. – deceased (suicide),
                       two children (Louis, Lorrie);
                       Beth Ann Johnson – married,
                       two children (Annie, Kate);
                       Mark – estranged, three children
                       (Mark, Michelle, Michael)

It was not until she was twenty-eight that she decided to track his whereabouts. She knew he had moved from their hometown, but she had no idea where, and she was not about to ask his whereabouts of anyone from back there-and-then. No one will ever be able to say she had shown the least bit of interest in or knowledge of her devil. Her only recourse was a PI.

Mr. Williams, Sr. was warm, friendly, and gentle – not at all what she expected a private investigator to be. He never asked her why she wanted the information and, after the first meeting, they never met again but remained in touch only through the annual report that was sent to her post office box – listed pseudonymously – which she maintained solely for that one piece of mail. (Choosing her *nom de guerre* was the most difficult part of the deception. It had to be meaningful and strong enough to endure what lay ahead. She settled on Abigail Adams.) He accepted her name and address as pukka with no comment on the historical coincidence. She always suspected, however, that he suspected. Every year – for thirty years – she visited the postal box just once and always with a warm and light heart as though she were anticipating a letter from a dear and treasured friend.

Year after year – for thirty years – the report would arrive around the first of September – her birthday – with slight changes from the previous year's report: each new item – divorced, deceased, wife remarried, estranged – brought her a sense of satisfaction as she envisioned the pain such life events brought him. Ah, she would think, but this pain is nothing in relation to what he has in store.

Through the years, she concentrated on making her life rich with a loving family, meaningful career, and loyal friends. The good life she created for herself (in spite of the horrors and humiliations of those two years of her childhood) was, to her knowledge, not the "living life well" that brings the sought for revenge, since he, in all likelihood, did not even remember her. She was known as a gentle and loving mother, friend, and community volunteer. Quiet – almost shy – she was liked by everyone who knew her. *She never has an unkind word about anyone.*

She had begun planning her revenge even before the abuse had stopped. She knew she could count on no one but herself for such judicial rectitude. When she had shyly told her mother that she did not like him; that he looked at her funny; that he made her feel icky; her mother had simply laughed and told her not to be silly. *Silly!*

And then the dripping looks progressed to murky words. Dark and dangerous. Wet, slimy, and slippery sounds spoken quietly and slyly for her ears only. *Don't you look precious today, Nora. Why, I swear, you're sweet enough to eat.* And he'd smile that loose-lipped, wet smile that both repulsed and fascinated her.

It was Easter Sunday and, although he was a Jew, he always spent the holidays with them. *Easter. Passover. What does it matter? We're all celebrating Spring. Here, have some more ham.* Her mother was never more jubilant than when serving Sunday dinner to a hungry crowd – unless it was a holiday Sunday dinner. *Nora, darling, will you bring in the rolls from the kitchen. That's the good girl.*

She could feel his lidded, lizard eyes on her and that sicky-icky feeling growled inside her stomach and made her palms moist and her eyes throb. *Why doesn't anyone else see what a scary man he is?*

Dinner was over and aunts, uncles, and cousins had said their loud good-byes. He was the only remaining guest, and he and Father were laughing in the parlor while watching Arnold Palmer do his magic on the golf course. Mother and Sissy were beginning to wash the dishes from which Nora was excused after she had helped clear the table.

Upstairs in her pretty pink and white room Nora was about to change out of her new Easter dress when she heard the frantic shouts downstairs; Sissy crying in pain, Mother shouting to get the car, Father yelling to hurry. By the time she reached the kitchen it had been decided. Father and Mother would rush Sissy to the emergency room for stitches in her cut and bleeding hand, and he would remain behind to watch over Nora.

But I want to go. Oh, Mommy, please let me go with you. Daddy, please. I don't want to stay here alone.

Don't be silly, Nora. He'll stay with you, and we'll be back soon. Sissy will be all right but we have to hurry. Now you be a good girl.

And they were gone, and he was closing the door behind them.

Fifty years ago. Plenty of time for her to plot her revenge. And now the plan was perfected, and she was ready.

Her flight to Maine was long and tiring, but she felt refreshed and relaxed when at last she arrived at Boston Logan, picked up her rental car, and began the two hour drive to Portland. She planned to return to Boston that night – after it was all over – and immediately return home. Her family would never know she had even left the city, let alone the state.

It was Spring – several days before Easter – and the trip north from Boston was pleasant. She had never been to New England and regretted she could not take some time to enjoy the scenery. Perhaps she would suggest a tour of New England for the annual family vacation. Yes, that would be pleasant. But for now she had business to attend.

The scenery – what there was of it – was lovely despite being jammed between too many houses, malls, factories, and office parks for such a small area. It lacked the drama and spirituality of the southwest where Mother Nature's hand, sweeping large, painted the spirit with tranquility, assurance, and warmth; excitement, Zen-esque silence, and vivificative energy. Surely, those who were forced to live in such crowed conditions on the outskirts of New England cities were emotionally impacted – grey, jaded, and stressed.

She found his office easily. On the corner of Longfellow and Maine, it was a converted nineteenth century Victorian home with high peaks and gables. Bright yellow with a dark green door, it looked the quintessential New England attempt at restoration of history. Revisionist history.

The pretty young receptionist showed her into his inner office. *Mrs. Hunt?* He approached her with his hand extended and a slippery smile on the lips she had all too often recalled over the past fifty years.

Hello, Mr. Robus. I'm sorry I'm late. The traffic from Boston was more than I had bargained for. She smiled and took his hand. This, she knew, would be the most difficult part.

Thirteen years older than her, he looked exactly as she knew he would look at 71: his whole had caught up with his loose and blubbery lips. His bulging, lizard eyes were pale, watery and without color. They didn't look at her as much as they slithered over her. At twenty-one he had looked and smelled oily, and at 71 he remained drenched in the slime and ooze drained from a long neglected engine. His voice was oily, phlegmatic, and cold – the sound of a garden slug and the warmth of a garden spade. She felt a chill and shuddered inadvertently.

Would you like a cup of coffee before we head out? You must be tired.

Actually, I was hoping we could see the house immediately so I could be back on the road and home before dark. She had told him she lived in Boston.

She had carefully perused his listings and chosen an unoccupied house. It was in a wooded area on the outskirts of the city. They would not be disturbed.

The house was a large farmhouse and still smelled of the recently departed occupants. It was damp and cold from being closed up through late winter and into this particularly cool spring, and he switched on the gas fireplace and went around the lower floor raising the shades to let in the sunlight.

"I'm pleased, but rather surprised you're working on Passover. I'm sure your family would rather have you home."

"Not at all. But how did you know I was Jewish?" He looked genuinely surprised.

That was stupid! Stupid, stupid, stupid. How did I let that slip? I've got to be more careful.

"Oh, I have neighbors named Robus who are Jewish, so I just assumed you would be too." She spoke casually and immediately changed the subject. "Oh, how lovely the gas fireplace is. And how convenient. Does it give off much heat?" She smiled pleasantly and moved toward the fireplace.

"In fact, I have one similar in my own home, and I'd be willing to guess this one would heat the entire downstairs. I believe there is another one in the dining room and between the two, I doubt you'd have to use the baseboard heat except in the coldest of weather." He began to move toward the dining room.

"The ride out was so long, I'm afraid I have to use the bathroom. I do hope they are working." She looked around toward doors that seemed likely.

"In winters hereabouts you wouldn't dare close off the heat for fear of pipes freezing, and we also left water running just to make sure. You can use the one off the kitchen, over there."

She walked through the country kitchen and entered the bathroom. In the mirror she startled herself with how calm she looked. And normal. She washed her hands and looked around for a towel on which to dry them. None was found so she patted them on the roll of toilet tissue.

Reaching into her large purse, she pulled out the gun. It was much heavier than she would have liked but certainly was impressive. "No doubt, he would be particularly impressed," she laughed to herself as she tucked it under her long wool scarf that draped down from her neck.

She loathed guns and was a strong advocate of stricter gun control. It never ceased to amaze her how the right-wing gun lobbies could ignore the fatality statistics from guns – statistics that increased every year. Two things came to her mind: ignorant machismo and money. In the end, everything was written in green ink.

He was gazing out a window when she re-entered the living room, his back to her. He was not a big man. Not as big as she recalled from her eight-year old's memory. He was, however, still a proud man. Straight posture – almost stiff. An expensive suit and a manicure. She wondered what he was thinking. What did pedophiles think when gazing out windows?

She had noticed his hands – which now hung limply by his side – while he was driving and had to force herself from staring at them. Those were the hands that altered her innocence. She used to say "stole" her innocence until her therapist encouraged her not to give him that power. Dr. Dickson. She had begun seeing her when she was old enough to choose her own. The innumerable therapists and counselors her parents had taken her to from her tenth year through high school were not Dr. Dickson. No. She knew a good therapist when she finally met one, and they were definitely no Dr. Dickson. She never told them of the sexual abuse. If her own mother had dismissed it (and her) when told, then surely one of these social workers fresh out of Social Work Training 101 would have no clue. She was convinced that Social Work was the major students chose when they knew they could not succeed in any more demanding profession. When her oldest daughter flirted with the idea of majoring in Social Work she had convinced her to first get an education, a proper education in philosophy and theology, the arts, history, psychology, mathematics, sciences, and, above all, literature. Then, once equipped with a modicum of education, if she still wanted to receive training in Social Work, go for it. By the time she was in her third year, she understood the difference between a social worker and a psychologist and opted for the latter.

Dr. Dickson restored her innocence – or at least guided her in the reclamation of it on her own. She helped her grow beyond the trauma and shame of victimhood. She was now ready to dump that trauma and shame where it belonged.

"Mr. Robus," she said in a soft voice. He turned from the brightness of the outside light and smiled at her before his eyes adjusted to the relative dimness inside and saw her holding a gun pointed directly at him.

"My, my, Mr. Robus, the look on your face at this moment is worth every effort I've made to find you. Surely you're not afraid of this little eight-year old girl who's sweet enough to eat?"

He looked uncomprehending, doltish, and confused. He forced a weak laugh. "Is this some kind of a joke?"

"That line is so predictable. How many times have we heard that line in B-rated movies? No, Mr. Robus, this is not some kind of a joke. It's not any kind of a joke. This is deadly serious. And, I repeat, most deadly." She smiled sweetly. "For you, that is. Not for me."

He blanched, and his eyes began to swim in watery excess. "Can I sit down?"

"Not on the sofa, Mr. Robus, on that chair over there. And, by the way, it's *may I,* not *can I.*"

As she walked round and round his chair with the duct tape, she thought of Garrison Keeler's duct tape shtick and smiled. *I doubt he'd use this duct tape story on his* Prairie Home Companion. She was a bit disappointed in his immediate acquiescence. She was hoping she would have to wave the gun around a bit and get tough. Just for the fun of it. But, no, he obeyed her every command. His whimpering, however, was very satisfying. "Odd," she thought.

"He has not asked who I am or why I'm doing this. He may not know who I am, but he certainly knows what I am and why I'm doing this. I'll bet there are lots and lots of little eight-year-old girls who simply run together in his evil mind. I'm just one of them, and it doesn't matter who I am. He knows!"

"All those little girls you've hurt through the years are in this room with you right now, Mr. Robus." He whimpered louder. And longer. "Do you hear me, Mr. Robus?"

"What are you going to do to me?"

Yes, he *knew* alright. Never even a "Who are you?" or "What are you talking about?" or "I don't know what this is all about." Yes, he *knew*.

"How many little girls are there, Mr. Robus? How many children have you filled with fear and shame and self-doubt? How many womyn now cower in the corners of life because of your evil?

"Do you know what *e pluribus unum* means, Mr. Robus? It's the motto of the United States: Out of Many, One. Well, Mr. Robus, at this moment, in this room, I am the One representing the Many. Remember that, Mr. Robus, *e pluribus unum*. Every child your slimy and sinister eyes have slithered over. Every child your depravity has deprived of innocence. Every little girl – and maybe little boys too, eh, Mr. Robus? – that your Minotaur-esque foul and filthy hands every touched. They are all in this room with me at this minute. And, they are all rejoicing in what is about to happen to you."

"Please." His voice was a pig squeal. "Please."

"Please? Please?" Her voice rose for the first time. "Please? Is that all you can say. Please? You don't even give a damn who I am 'cause your victims were all alike to you – without any identity. Only your conscienceless lust meant anything to you. We were simply tissue paper you wiped your sad and sorry ass with and threw away. We were disposable, valueless, forgettable. And you have the nerve to say, 'Please'?"

He was crying now. No sound came from his mouth, but his body heaved and shook and his eyes poured copious tears over his blubbery and contorted face. "I've got to go to the bathroom."

She stared at him and made no reply.

As she gazed down on him the hatred she felt was palpable. It encompassed her entire being, and she literally saw red: Red heat wavered in front of her eyes, and her body burned with a fire she had never before known. She thought she had hated him all these years, but what she now felt – the full force of her hatred –

was so overwhelming, so powerful, it literally took her breath away, and she gasped.

He looked up at her through his waterlogged eyes, and she saw it: not the terror or shock she expected but . . . what? What was it she saw in those sinister and cloven-hoofed eyes? Peace? Serenity? Calmness and Contentment? Not quite. But what? Migawd, its Gratitude! That's what shone through the saline sop. Gratitude! Surely that couldn't be.

Suddenly it occurred to her: he wanted to be punished. Yes, *wanted* to be punished. And, he wanted *her* to punish him. Now *that's* some kind of a joke! She imagined him, over the years, buying the punishment he craved from prostitutes – probably child prostitutes. But the punishment *she* could give him would be the ultimate release. The ultimate *mea culpa*. She'd be damned if she'd deliver absolution to this beast. It was redemption he wanted from her. He saw her as the deliverer of the salvation he craved in his elderly years.

She felt numb. Robbed. Tricked. Now what? She thought of *Le Miserable's* Javert. Was she Javert? A life spent in misguided pursuit? Surely he was no Jean Valjean. And what of all the Cosettes? If they were truly in the room with her, she needed their guidance. Now.

The gun was still in her hand, but the heft of it had dragged her arm down by her side. She lifted the gun with both hands and pointed at his face, specifically his nose. His eyes shone with the light of the confessor leaving the confessional, but she would be damned if she would serve as his confessor. She would not assign him ten Hail Mary's and ten Our Fathers.

He heard the click of the gun being cocked, and he sighed as he released, simultaneously, his bladder and bowels. The sigh was in anticipation of complete release and cleansing which she would not provide.

Slowly she lowered the gun, and the shine in his eyes diminished. "You stink," she said quietly as she walked out leaving him sitting in his own filth.

Polly

She could feel her life drifting from her – gentle, painless. A misty tenderness for her death warmed her as she lay in the bloodied mud of this Mexican battlefield. Around her were twelve or twenty other soldiers: some dead, others sobbing, groaning, pleading for Life to maintain a grip on their beings.

The death throes of her fellow infantrymen, the distant sound of cannons, and the closer sound of muskets did not penetrate the cocoon of silence that embraced her. Blessedly, none of her senses relayed to her consciousness the existence of their stimuli. Spared the putrid stench, ghastly sights, and acrid taste of this dying field, she was aware only of a profound sense of serenity.

She now knew that soldiering was more than dressing the part. Her brother's uniform skimmed only the surface of her being: his passion for the sport failed to penetrate her psyche. He would have enjoyed these past five months of battle. It should be he not her experiencing this soldier's death in this soldier's arena. He would have imbued it with some glory; some pride.

He had been so excited at the prospect of war with Mexico and, oh, so handsome in his blue uniform. He had been in northern Mexico less than a month when he succumbed to the fever. The letter from his commander, "Old Rough and Ready" Zachary Taylor, was not specific as to the ailment, only to the certainty of his death.

She attempted to comfort her mother who was beyond comforting. The War of 1812 had taken her mother's father, and she tried to imagine her mother, as a little girl, trying to comfort her own mother. Was the loss of her father greater or less than the loss of her son? She wondered but did not ask.

America was less than 100 years old and had already aggressively invaded her neighbors to the north and south. Fighting the British in Canada and the Mexicans in their own country seemed to her to be . . . well, arrogant – Manifest Destiny, indeed!

"More like Manifest Greed, if you ask me," she shouted at her twin when he proudly announced he had signed on with the volunteers. She was furious he would leave her for this adventure south.

Her fury was mixed with envy which made her even more furious. Yet again he would experience something interesting while she was forced to remain in Virginia playing the lady. It wasn't fair. The danger inherent in his adventure never occurred to her.

The letter from Washington fueled and incensed her anger at Death for robbing her brother of his adventure. The ignominy of his death did not escape her and added to her rage.

When news reached Virginia that Major General Winfield Scott finally succeeded in convincing President Polk that an invasion was the best way to win the war with Mexico, she knew immediately what she would do.

It amazed her how easy it was to secure a uniform in her brother's name. With hair shorn and in his britches, she would challenge even her mother to distinguish her from her twin. She fled Virginia to join "Polk's War," as unpopular as it was, not for any sense of patriotism, but as her personal memorial to her twin brother.

As her awareness of Death's imminence embraced her, her mind drifted: She found herself obsessing on General Santa Anna's wooden leg. Since landing in Mexico in March, she was more aware of her feet and legs than ever in her life. Four straight months of marching from the coast to . . . well, to here: the muddy yard of a Catholic convent but a few miles from Mexico City. Would it have been more or less difficult with a leg that she could remove at night?

After the Battle of Cerro Gordo, with the Mexicans in chaotic retreat leaving behind cannons, muskets, and even Santa Anna's wooden leg – surely he had more than one – her comrades were at once ecstatic at the rousing defeat of the enemy and disappointed it meant the probable end to the fighting and their hopes of seeing the legendary Halls of Montezuma. No one expected Santa Anna to regroup his army and bring the fighting right to the gates of his capital.

She saw the irony in her dying at the hands, not of the tawny skinned soldiers she was sent to kill, but at the hands of other Americans. Granted, they were just barely Americans, only recently emigrated from Ireland; but still and all, they sailed from New Orleans for this exotic land wearing the same blue uniform as did she.

San Patricios they were called: the Saint Patricks. They even had their own flag proudly displaying the Celtic harp. The name rolled gently around in her head, *"San Patricios."* She could understand the Mexicans wanting to kill her but why these new Americans? What had motivated them to turn against their own countrymen and fight at the side of Santa Anna's troops?

It was rumored that her commander, General Twiggs, hated the San Patricios more than he hated the Mexicans. He was determined not to leave Mexico without capturing or killing the eighty odd traitors. His ill-concealed hatred did nothing to relieve the widespread prejudice of Catholic soldiers that was rampant among the rank and file. To be Catholic was to be suspect.

It was pure luck – for Twiggs, not the traitors – that the convent where the San Patricios were hiding was directly in the path of his route to join the other brigades at Churubusco. Despite their sparse numbers, the American traitors fiercely fought capture.

The face of the Irishman who brought her down was sad and beautiful. He was no more than a year or two older than her – nineteen at the most. For a brief moment before lunging his bayonet into her right side she saw a shock of recognition in his brilliant blue eyes. Their eyes had met, and she read hesitancy in the cloud that dimmed the brilliance of the blue. She smiled to herself as she recalled him closing his eyes before striking.

In slow motion the bayonet punctured the skin just beneath her rib cage and smoothly sunk into her soft innards. It found its way to her spinal column, and there met momentary resistance. An extra thrust – almost gentle – severed the resister, and she instantly collapsed forward onto the boy. She heard him cry out as he struggled to extract the bayonet: "Oh, Jesus, Mary, and Joseph," he sobbed in a strange, tongue-curling brogue, "Help me."

He was kneeling beside her then as he frantically tried to wrestle the bayonet from her body. Again their eyes met – his sobbing ceased, and the fear and pain in his eyes melted away to be replaced once again by the beautiful sadness.

Gently he rolled her onto her back, never taking his eyes from hers. The bayonet came out easily then and, without looking at it, he placed it behind him. His voice was tender: soft and warm. "I'm sorry."

Without moving from her side, he scooped two handfuls of the clay like mud onto the orifice left by the bayonet. Tenderly he took each of her hands in his. Before placing them on her chest she watched him examine them. Again he looked in her eyes and again back to her hands. "I'm sorry," he repeated. He reluctantly forced his gaze from hers, hesitated less than the length of his sigh, gathered his musket and now bloodied bayonet, and fled.

She had known him but a brief few minutes, yet she knew him intimately. Had he been taken alive, this sensitive and loving tergiversator? Would he think of her as he faced the inevitable execution? Did he understand she forgave him? Was he as relieved as was she to be removed from the killing game?

The desert sky was unlike any she had seen in Virginia: close and as blue as the eyes of her reluctant killer. The billowing cumulus clouds, a fleecy blanket covering her terminal moments, drifted above her. One revealed a one-legged giant and another a ship in full sail. She closed her eyes before the giant disappeared and the ship sank into the bluest of seas.

CARNIVAL

She moved slowly, sensuously through her gardens: a priestess amidst her worshippers blessing them with her eyes. The late October gale the night before had left the last of the summer blooms ravaged, the stems bare, the ground littered with the brown and mushy leaves. The northeastern winds off the Bay of Fundy whipped over the little island matching in their extreme velocity the extreme of the Bay's forty-foot tides.

The morning was calm following the thunderous drama of the previous night. The soft, muted sound of the diminished waves lapping the stony beach below the bluff on which she roamed was a chamber music meant for small spaces. They sighed in gratitude of surviving the juggernaut mountains of water that ravaged their peaceful beach in the night leaving them at the mercy of Nature's fury.

She recited Emily Dickinson aloud to the spring bulbs – warm fetuses beneath the frosted ground – and to the stark stems that clutched the earth ever hopeful they, too, will regain Paradise in the spring:

> An awful Tempest mashed the air –
> The clouds were gaunt, and few –
> A Black – as of a Spectre's Cloak
> Hid Heaven and Earth from view.
> The creatures chuckled on the Roofs –
> And whistled in the air –
> And shook their fists –
> And gnashed their teeth –
> And swung their frenzied hair.
> The morning lit – the Birds arose –
> The Monster's faded eyes
> Turned slowly to his native coast –
> And peace – was Paradise!

Autumn had come early and brilliant this year, remaining only long enough to deliver the bitter news of winter in the deceptively gay envelope of gold, orange, and scarlet leaves. (The sparrow and humming bird, never caught unawares, never deceived, had left for warmer climes weeks ago.) This region that bore the brunt of winter's bleak, barren, and unforgiving personality never failed to be hoodwinked by the colors of autumn. For the week or ten days of Autumn's fiery symphony, natives were lulled into believing that Mother Nature had blessed them – above all others – with her beauty. The pallid grey death mask of winter was hidden in their memories by the peacock foliage of fall: Mother Nature's camouflage in which she disguised her true intent as she armed herself with the bombs she would drop once the victims were distracted by her siren songs of color. The death knells of ice, snow, slush, grays-on-grays-on-grays, and time that stretched interminably from the first, depressing frosts of November through the last, exhausting frosts of April.

November was well chosen as the month of death and today was the eve of The Day of the Dead: Halloween; when the diaphanous veil between life and death is at her sheerest. Donning dominos, the ghouls would venture forth at dark, roaming the streets demanding treats with which to accompany their return to the tombs of winter. Treats to see them through to the Carnival – the *carni val* – when new dominos would celebrate the end of winter – death of death – and the resurrection of spring.

Halloween and Carnival – The Day of the Dead and Shrovetide – bookends supporting death.

The succubus of death evident in her garden was, like the ghouls of Halloween and the revelers of Carnival, only a mask, a domino, a false face hiding the life that throbbed beneath the soil – the soul of her garden.

She was a mirror to her garden; lifeless, cold, and withered. She wondered if her mien, like that of the garden, was only a domino of death hiding throbbing life deep in her soul. Or was she truly dead with no hope of daffodils and tulips breaking through her icy spirit come Shrovetide?

She gazed over the now calm water, across the floating triple mounds of The Wolves to the New Brunswick mainland. The Wolves, islands mid-way between her wee island and Saint John on the mainland, were reassuringly and clearly visible. No fog devoured their black and steady presence. She felt grounded by their constancy; her electric energy controlled by their rooted circuit.

Autumn – the harbinger of death – often left her empty. Spiritually ravaged as appeared to be both her annuals and perennials. Would she yet again prove to be perennial as were her day lilies, tulips, peonies, lilacs, iris, astelba, and Shasta daisies? And her roses; her beloved roses. Or would she join the ranks of her petunias, labelia, ageratum, nicotiana, geraniums, and alyssum? She certainly could never aspire to the ranks of the innumerable evergreens that danced around the cottage, embraced the gardens, and laughed at the changing seasons before running down the bluff toward the beach – their regal spires ever more distant as they descended from the heights of her bluff. Firs, pines, spruce soaring toward eternity, be it blue or grey.

Given a choice she would include herself in the class of the wildflowers – most particularly the lupine. She would *be* lupine. *Lupinus.* Beautiful, bright colors: pink, purple, blue, red. And generous with reproduction – spreading beauty in ever-wider spiraling ranges of space never knowing where – how far – her fertile seed will flourish.

She smiled to herself when she thought of the charming quote of Eleanor Roosevelt when a rose was honored with her name: "I was honored to have such a beautiful rose named after me until I read the description of this particular rose: hardy, beautiful, thrives in sun and partial shade, not good in bed."

She shuddered with a chill that suddenly blew in from the Bay. The Wolves had disappeared – devoured by a living fog that was drifting in soft and silent banks toward the beach. Like the lupine that were consumed by the specters of autumn but resurrected in the spring, she knew that the Wolves would be regurgitated when the fog was sated and returned to the depths of the Atlantic. As the lupine would thrust their spires through the soil once the Carnival announced the end of death and the resurrection of life, The Wolves, grounded to the sea, would outwit the fog and prevail. For now both Lupine and Wolves were protecting themselves by withdrawing into the warmth of their souls.

And what of her protective soul? Born and raised an islander, she knew the terror of moving beyond the perimeters of shore. The mainland was for mainlanders. The island was for islanders. Mainland or island, the Canadian winters chilled the soul and threatened the annual resurrection. She turned with one last fond glance at her slumbering garden and returned to the cottage.

The setting sun washed the eastern horizon with pink. The Bay, so violent not twenty four hours ago, was subdued and pacific. It was this sea Rachel Carson knew when she wrote, "For all at last returns to the sea – to Oceanus, the ocean river, like the ever-flowing stream of time, the beginning and the end." She decided, for her, this sea that shone pink through her cottage windows would be her beginning.

Halloween past, All Saints Day dawns, and the eyes of the cottage blink closed as she draws the blinds, locks the doors, bestows one last blessing on her garden, and follows the sparrows and humming birds to warmer climes – and color. To anti-death. To *carni val.*

The Offender

She paused only momentarily as she put her hand on the door knob to the small, windowless room. Each Tuesday, for the past nine years, she had entered this room precisely at 7:00. This evening, however, she sensed something. But what? And with which sense? Smell? Sound? Taste? She felt a flutter of anxiety which was most unusual for her. From whence it came she did not know, but her intuition never failed.

She advised her patients – female survivors (it was no longer acceptable to acknowledge they were recovering victims) and the offenders alike – to listen more closely to their intuition: to add their intuition to their intellect as an integral part of their knowledge formation.

"In the name of my intellect and my intuition comes insight." As in the Church of Rome's self-blessing in the names of the father, son, and holy ghost, she lightly touched her forehead, lower stomach (in the region of her uterus) and, indicating insight, gently ran her right fingertips up her throat, smoothly completing the blessing with her palm up in front of her chin.

Yes, she had learned to trust her instincts – her intuition – which she knew resided not in her heart but in her uterus. She could feel the power of her uterus as many could feel the power of their hearts. It gave her courage, comfort, and confidence.

Her agency was one of the few in the city offering treatment for sex offenders, and she was among the even fewer womyn psychologists facilitating therapy groups for criminal male offenders. Rapists, adult child molesters, criminal voyeurs, exhibitionists, public masturbators, child pornographers (which she saw as a redundancy), and any number of other criminal sexual deviants.

Invariably the offenders were childhood victims of abuse themselves. If not direct sexual abuse, then physical, emotional, or spiritual abuse. The violence of their childhood converted to the violence of their adulthood. While little girls who were sexually or physically abused frequently developed into womyn who turned the violence inward toward themselves, little boys victimized by childhood violence became adults who projected the violence outward toward others. Womyn punished themselves with compulsive excesses of food, drugs, violent relationships, sex, shopping, spending, caretaking, martyrdom. Men punished the world with homicides, domestic violence, random pugilism, rape, arson, war.

She took a deep breath, consciously erased any stress from her face, turned the knob and entered the room.

Tonight there were eight members present; seven long-time patients and a new member she had yet to meet. Art, a fat and middle-aged Phoenix attorney, was on life-time probation for sexually abusing his three daughters; Conrad was barely out of his teens and was on probation after spending six months in jail at 18 for having sex with his 15-year-old girlfriend. Her parents had him arrested as the only way they could stop their daughter from seeing him. Alphonso: in and out of prison since he was a kid, he struggled with his misogyny which manifested itself in the rapes of three elderly womyn over the past twenty to thirty years; and those were only the rapes he thus far has acknowledged. Francis was the only member who was in group of his own volition, but that was only because he had not yet been caught exposing himself to young girls. He was frightened enough by the last close call to seek help. Daniel and Mañuel: both regressed pedophiles, both on long-term probation, and both recovering alcoholics. Mañuel was still married to the mother of his children, but he was not able to see the children so their mother allowed the state to take them so she could stay with Mañuel. Daniel was separated from his kids and saw them only under supervision. Joshua: sad, lonely, beautiful, bi-sexual Joshua. At 38 he was beginning to come to terms with the probability that he was a fixed pedophile and would most likely have to be on probation and in therapy for life. They were chatting quietly among themselves when she entered, and upon seeing her, they smiled hellos and settled into their seats. She knew each of them so very well and cared deeply for each of them.

The new member was sitting one seat removed on each side from the other members and was silently looking down at his hands. He briefly looked up at her – his eyes dull and his expression blank – then resumed his slumped posture and examination of his hands.

She had read his intake forms: Willard Franks, 72, Jewish, recently released from 7 years in prison, divorced, five children, college educated, currently living in a half-way house on the outskirts of the city. He was dressed casually but expensively in beige khaki pants and a dark brown Polo shirt. His only jewelry was a watch that seemed new and fashionable. Clean shaven, his grey hair was short and styled with mousse, and his nails – on the hands from which he could not take his eyes – were manicured. The musky scent of aftershave – unusual in this group – she assumed was his. Slender but muscular, he was deceptively young looking and could pass for being in his late fifties or early 60s.

"Good evening, gentlemen." Her voice was soft, deep, and warm with rounded edges that smoothed one word into the next with a gentle enunciation. A kind voice yet strong and sure; self-confident, quietly commanding. A voice with expectations of being heard and taking no truck with disrespectful interruptions. A voice one immediately trusted.

The men were relaxed and attentive. They knew the routine and felt comfortable – perhaps more comfortable than they felt elsewhere in their lives.

"Before we begin, I'd like us all to welcome our new member, Mr. Frank." While members of the survivor groups were not identified by their surnames, the offenders were required to do so. Most of the offenders were referred to group by court order with the mandate to register as sex offenders, notify their immediate neighbors and their employers of their status, and participate in a variety of recovery programs.

"Mr. Frank, would you like to be called Willard, or do you prefer a nickname?"

Without looking up at either her or the group he whispered, "Will. I'm called, Will." His voice was neither friendly nor defiant, but resigned and sad. Very sad.

"Hey, Will," "Welcome, man," "Gladjahere, guy." The welcomes from the others were good-natured and sincere, and Will acknowledged them with a brief nod. Mañuel – the closest to him – raised his hand in a high-five gesture, and Will, with barely a glance, half-heartedly responded.

The session opened with the usual mantra: "I'm Dr. Dickson, and I'm here to assist you in your understanding that what you *did* was evil – very evil – but *you* are not evil." The two-hour session progressed smoothly. Much of the time was spent on a problem Mañuel had run into at work and on last week's journal writing assignment.

Although by nine – the end of the session – Will had not uttered a word, he had, after the first fifteen minutes or so, slowly begun to loosen the intensity of his interest in his hands and began paying attention to the discussions. As each of the members read excerpts from his journal of his week's activities, Will was slowly being drawn into the circle. Although he never spoke – and never made eye contact with any of the speakers – he was engaged in the discussions and some light began to glimmer from his eyes, his posture relaxed, and his hands no longer clutched each other.

"Until next week, gentlemen, and you all know your assignments. Will, although you were excused from participating this week, it being your first, please be prepared to participate next week."

That night she slept fitfully. Something about Will troubled her. She re-read his intake chart after group but nothing stood out of the ordinary – if the details of a child molester's life could ever be considered *ordinary*. But there was definitely something. She just couldn't put her finger on it. There was something nagging at her instincts – and her instincts were never wrong.

Over the next several weeks, Will slowly unraveled his history, and the group became *his* group, and he became a full-fledged member of the group. He was open and forthcoming and friendly. His sense of humour was appreciated by the group, and they all liked and trusted him. She liked him. But still there was *something*.

"Never ignore your instincts," she preached over and over to all her patients, "and never rely solely on your intellect. The one reinforces the other, and together they won't be wrong."

She found herself testing her own theory over the ensuing weeks. Carefully observing Will, she assessed him to be a committed member of the group and a good candidate for recovery. This is what she reported to his probation officer. And yet . . . the nagging doubt continued.

Sleep was never a problem for her, and her many years of therapy had helped her leave her childhood nightmares – most particularly *the* nightmare – behind. And then it returned. Not every night but at least two or three times a week – usually mid-week, Tuesdays, Wednesdays, and Thursdays; occasionally Mondays. Strange, she thought. It has been years since I've been terrorized by the nightmare. Why now? It left her tired, irritable, and reluctant to go to sleep.

She was eight when the nightmare started haunting her sleep, shortly after her father died. She never told her mother about it but kept it as her personal terror through her teens and into her college years. When finally she began seeing a therapist, she did not need the therapist to interpret it for her. It was all too evident from whence it sprung: it was definitely from the other secret she kept from her mother.

The shame of the other secret seeped into her eight-year old soul and devoured her eight-year old joy. It increased exponentially as she moved through her teens and colored her world paradigm with a slimy darkness, a throbbing, hateful distrust. This secret – this shame – finally brought her to the therapist, and this shameful secret motivated her selection of career: a feminist psychologist specializing in the treatment of sexual abuse.

The nightmare was always the same, although sometimes she woke before the ending; sweating, panting, and clawing at her bedcovers. Often she would be forced to change the sheets because of the spreading wet patch in the center of the bed. Her mother never commented on her bed-wetting but quietly placed a rubber sheet, which she used through her teens, between her mattress and bottom sheet.

She is floating on a massive snow drift. The snow is warm and clean, and she is in her prettiest frock: lavender with white daisies and a bow that ties in the back. She is alone except for a hummingbird that hovers by her side. She can hear the beating of the bird's heart as it expends the enormous energy to keep itself in one place. She is happy and laughing until she notices that her shoes are all dirty. She smells the filth that covers them, and it smells like the outhouse at their cottage in the mountains. She is crying now and the humming bird disappears. It is getting dark and she is frightened. She tries to walk off the snow drift, but her feet are missing, and she can't move. The snow becomes cold and covered with the same filth that covered her shoes. She cries harder, and the snowdrift turns into the irrigation ditch behind her house. The sun is shining, but it is cold and blue and smells bad, and she is scared of the man who is telling her to be quiet. Stop crying. Shut up. She sees his hand moving up, up, up in slow motion before it comes down, down, down to slap her. The ring he is wearing is shining in the sun, and she is hypnotized by its beauty. It is a horse's head, and the eyes are green emeralds. Its nostrils are flared and black – shiny black onyx. The horse smiles at her, and she knows he will not let the man hurt her. The hand continues to descend, and the horse disappears into the terrifying darkness of her pain.

Tuesday at seven and the nagging anxiety returns, as it has every Tuesday since Will joined the group. She is accustomed to it now and impatiently tells herself to "get a grip" as she enters the small, windowless group room. *Is my intuition no longer infallible?*

The men – nine of them this week – are gathered around Will. "Dr. Dickson, you've gotta see this neat ring. Will's father gave it to him when he was a kid, and his ex-wife kept it for him until he got out of prison." Will is smiling and proudly holds up his manicured hand. "Except while in prison, I've worn this every day of my life since I graduated from eighth grade. It's great to have it back."

She knew. Without even looking at it, she knew. She stood quietly for a moment – non-plussed. Her voice: That gift she so nourished and utilized to control the rush and whirl of the world. She had to drag it up from the depths of her soul. She had to say something. "Are you okay, Doc?" The men were suddenly quiet. Concerned. All eyes on her. They had never seen her pale. Never seen her anything but the Dr. Dickson they trusted, admired. They depended on her to always be what they came to expect each Tuesday. The only element in their shattered lives they knew would be stable, steadfast, unshakable. The constance of Gibraltar. Their one hope for diminishing their shame and rejoining the world of the wholesome and healthy. The accepted.

She felt herself stagger, and she gripped the door knob behind her. Her mind was a fiery white heat. Her uterus felt heavy: humid and bulging. Her heart was cold as a blue sun. She shuddered.

Her voice formed in her bulging uterus and rose slowly up her spine by-passing her heart and lungs. When it emerged – high pitched, cracked and uncontrolled – it shattered like icicles falling from eaves and hitting the sidewalk. "Excuse me."

She found her way back to her office. Lacking the energy to walk around to her desk chair, she melted into one closest to the door in front of her desk. Facing her empty desk chair she howled silently and cruelly. Her uterus burst opening a flood of pain that floated before her eyes as she collapsed her head into her hands.

What you did was evil – very evil – but you are not evil. How often had she repeated that mantra to her offenders. And meant it.

It was the foundation of her philosophy, without which she would not be able to effectively – and compassionately – treat that category of men who are the most hated in society. Without which she would not be able to help them cope with the guilt of their actions and shed the pain of their shame. Guilt and shame. Two very different burdens. Her offenders – yes, she considered them *hers* – were not evil. *Guilt,* she frequently reminded them, *is when you feel remorse for something you did. Shame is when you feel remorse for something you are. Guilt you can live with. Shame will kill you.*

It was close to nine when she returned to the small, windowless room. She was not certain the men would still be there, but they were. Waiting. Where else would they be – where else could they go – on a Tuesday between seven and nine? Subdued – almost frightened. Their eyes were heavy with glazed moisture; the condensation of their weeping memories collected on the window of their souls.

"Good evening, gentlemen." Her voice was back. Their Dr. Dickson was back. "Please forgive my indisposition, and thank you for waiting so patiently. I'm feeling better now." She felt calm: her uterus was warm and comfortable, and her mind was clear. Her voice, like the horse, was resurrected in all its beauty and power. "Now, where were we? Oh, yes. Will, you were showing me your ring."

She smiles gently as she gazes at the horse with the green emerald eyes and the shiny black onyx nostrils, knowing that, after all, the beautiful stallion would not let the man hurt her. *My intuition is never wrong.*

Moonpath

She sat naked in the center of the skiff listening to the silence of the night and tasting the warm, golden honey of the moon as it lit a path from horizon to shore. The skiff rocked gently just outside the moonpath's light. She gazed at the brilliant path with reverence and love, the path on which she would walk toward her fate.

How often she had gazed at the rising moon and her shimmering stream of gold across the lake she could not estimate. The cabin, built by her grandfather, was the heart of the family's summers since before her birth. It was witness to her first summer's infancy being nursed by her mother in a wooden Adirondack chair at the water's edge; her fearless dash as a toddler for the magnetic pull of the water only to be scooped up by her ever-vigilant Mother preventing her from rejoining the water, yet; her swift and aggressive plunge into the world of "swimmer" allowing for rejoining the water sans succumbing to its primal call. It witnessed her first summer romance: the romance that began and ended at the water's edge with Daniel; her life-mate, soul-mate, and friend of 42 years. And, as the circle closed, it witnessed the first summer's infancy of her daughter, Danielle, as she nursed her in the same wooden Adirondack chair at the water's edge. And now it would witness her return to the watery womb at the end of the golden moonpath.

The serenity of the night permeated her soul, her heart, and her memories: Her uterus, if not buried long ago, would also have absorbed the serene silence and light of the moon-lit lake. She briefly wondered if the Energies of the Universe were able to reach the spirit of her uterus in its burial place beneath the yellow rose bush in her garden on shore. She longed to believe it would.

She found the long "i" in *suicide* distasteful and far more preferred the term *planned passage*: her intentional Canadian pronunciation gave a gentle and soft sound to the first "a" in *passage*. Yes, her planned passage would be gentle, peaceful, and serene. After considering other means, she rejected drugs as being too removed from nature. Wrist slitting or guns were never even considered, as the violence repelled her and brought too close to mind the current events of this sad and battered world. So it was she settled upon leaving the world as she entered it; with the cleansing essence of water, the water that once lubricated her entrance into this world, now would lubricate her departure.

Only ten months ago thoughts of planning her passage were far from her consciousness. The onset of her illness with its inevitable painful slide into a long and obscene death came suddenly. Doctors, tears, more doctors, tests, confirmations, more tears and more confirmations. No doubt: Within a year the deterioration of body and mind would commence and continue for three to five years of progressively more pain, loss of bodily control and consciousness, humiliation, expense, and anguish. No remedy. No hope of a reversal.

Life had always been her choice. Not Death. Yet here she was consciously and conscientiously choosing Death. She could not help but think of Ann Patchett. Not of her poetically sensuous *Bel Canto,* but her memoir of her 17-year friendship with the brilliant Lucy Grealy who died of an overdose of heroin in December 2002 at the age of 39. Ann was Lucy's best friend and wrote of her: Lucy "had a nearly romantic relationship with Death. She had beaten it out so many times that she was convinced she could go and kiss it all she wanted and still come out on the other side . . . ."

Unlike Lucy, she had never romanced Death. Quite the contrary. Rather, she thrilled to the romance of Life. The unpredictable twists and turns that Life takes with surprises at every juncture. But this irreversible illness, her final surprise, introduced her to the concept of kissing Death. Not to simply flirt with the intent of coming "out on the other side" but with the knowledge that it was the final kiss of her life; the Kiss of Judas. She did not fear kissing Death. She feared only not being able to control her thoughts as she approached Death's welcoming and loving arms.

She must not allow thoughts of violence, hatred, and ignorance to partake of these, her most intimate and personal moments. George Bush, Iraq, Rwanda. Homophobia, religious fundamentalism, racism. American chauvinism, poverty, war. Pseudo-professional ethics, classism, sexism, and anti-intellectualism. The Sudan, mean-spirited neighbors, her incestuous brother-in-law. They had obsessed and diminished her life. She must not let them diminish her death. She *would not* let them diminish her death.

The skiff's wooden seat felt warm; still radiating the rays of the summer sun. It was just long enough for the three of them to comfortably share. Buddha on her right, and Kali on her left. She pulled each of them closer to her so they lightly touched her thighs. The twine she had carefully wrapped around each statue was neatly coiled beneath them under the seat.

She had considered carefully which of her many gods she would take on her moon path journey. Buddha was a given. He embraced her throughout her life, seen her through moral, physical, spiritual, and intellectual crises. He, more than the others, would comfort and guide her as she prepared for her final journey.

Ganesh was considered, but instead she chose Kali: Creator and Destroyer. Destroyer and Creator. Kali who taught her the need to destroy life in order to nurture life. She would destroy her own life to nurture and protect their lives; Daniel, the sweetness of her heart, and Danielle, the fruit of her womb – the same womb that was destroyed in creating Danielle's life.

Yes, Kali would not only understand, but she would fully support her decision to destroy her life (what little there was left of it) to nurture and protect the life and spirit of her beloved two. They may not fully understand, but Kali would – *does*. She would not allow her death agonies to harm the spirits of her most spiritual life-mate or daughter.

With the oars neatly tucked along the inner sides of the skiff, she let her fingers lightly propel her into the warmth of the moonpath. Her fingers made barely a ripple in the black water and when the tip of the skiff crossed into the moonpath she let the skiff gently drift with the gathered, mild momentum. Spotlighted in the moonpath, she could see clearly the chipped blue and white paint of the skiff which had been freshly painted that spring – as it had every spring in her memory – and would be painted again next spring. Her physical absence would not halt the seasonal family trek to the cabin. They would be sad at her absence but not dispirited by a long and obscene death. Her spiritual presence would be with them through their grieving.

It was her spiritual presence she most cherished – both in Life and Death. The energy of Good she consciously tried to generate for the Universe. The energy of Love she knew would remain behind when she departed. The energy of Honest Intellect that came not from formal education but the life-long quest for truth and knowledge. The Good and the Love and the Honest Intellect were made manifest in the hearts, minds, and souls of her beloved two and, perhaps to a lesser degree, in the beings of her closest friends and many of her patients. That, alone, was the way the Universe would eventually heal: as the energies of Good and Love and Intellect spiraled in ever wider parameters from the hearts and souls of the good and the loving and the intellectual. The ignorance, hate, and divisiveness of fundamentalist religiosity frightened her, and its rapidly spreading prevalence world wide – most particularly among radical Christians, Jews, and Moslems – left her saddened and disheartened. Yet her faith in the power of an all-inclusive spirituality – one that neither judged others as evil because of their differing world paradigms nor damned those they did not understand to what they envisioned as a literal Hell – remained steadfast. Constant was her belief that spirituality would prevail in the destruction of the ignorance, hatred, and evil spread by the downward spiral of fundamentalist religiosity.

She caressed the heads of both Buddha and Kali and bent down to tie Buddha's cord to her right ankle and Kali's to her left. Lifting each in an arm, she stood for a moment and gazed first at the shore where the outline of the cabin was dimly visible in the moonlight. Her beloved two were asleep inside, and the enormity of love she had for them left her breathless. She could taste the honey sweetness and smell the rich, musky earth her love emitted. The power of such love could never die and would forever reproduce in the ages that stretched into the future.

The moon was rising and getting smaller as the moonpath was widening and becoming more silver than gold. She turned from the cabin and gazed at the moon for the last time. She felt at once calm and excited; sad and grateful. More vibrantly alive than she had since the onset of her illness.

The skiff barely swayed as she serenely stepped over the side onto the moonpath.

Aristotle

She awakened her partner, as she did every morning, with nose to nose resuscitation. Delicate as was her touch, it never failed to accomplish its intent: stirring, a groan, a few moments of that delicious scratching behind her ears and, finally, breakfast.

For her, the morning routine never varied. Breakfast was a half tray of Sheba: the remainder refrigerated for dinner. She refused anything but Sheba, despite her partner's attempts to introduce her to a more varied menu. It wasn't that she intentionally wanted to be finicky but simply that she was a culinary conservative: introduced to Sheba as a kitten, she tried – and judged unworthy – the innumerable menu alternatives offered over the years.

Despite breakfast and dinner being from the same tray, they were distinctly different in presentation. Breakfast, from the freshly opened tray, was warm and moist while dinner, having been stored in the refrigerator for hours, was cold and slightly dry, though every bit as delectable as was breakfast. An ordinary cat, a gross gourmand, may not detect the difference: she was a gourmet and relished the subtle distinctions in her meals. She greatly appreciated her partner's efforts to vary the flavors from day to day. If she served turkey one day, she thoughtfully offered beef the following day with duck or white fish later in the week. It was those seemingly minor considerations that bound their partnership with love and mutual respect. She was convinced no cat had a better partner.

Following breakfast Partner was free to pursue her own interests for the day. As for Aristotle, she had decisions to make that were dependent upon the season: in the spring and summer, the morning sun came through the kitchen and library windows, while in the autumn and winter, when there was sun at all, it could be found in the bedrooms and living room. Each room offered its peculiar charms for her morning nap. Today she chose the library where her favorite lounge was in the crease of Partner's unabridged dictionary that lay open on the table near the window. The oversized book smelled good: it reminded her of the cellar she sometimes visited on exceptionally hot days, and lying in the deep crease gave a sense of being hugged and protected by the two warm mountains of pages.

She was trilingual; fluent in Tactile, Scent, and Tone. As with her discriminating taste in food, she was equally discriminating in those with whom she chose to communicate. Partner frequently had friends in for the evening: some she tolerated with little interaction while some she actively disliked. Most, however, she liked and enjoyed participating in their evening conversations.

Reggie, loud and boisterous, tried hard to engage her in conversation. Aristotle suspected that he was using his obviously – to her – feigned love of cats to impress Partner with his desirability as a suitor. The thought of sharing Partner and their home with Reggie distressed her. She decided she must be more assertive in communicating her dislike of Reggie to protect Partner from an indiscriminate match. She did not like being rude to anyone, even Reggie, but she had noticed that Partner was spending increasingly more time with him: desperate times demand desperate measures, including rudeness.

Bob, on the other hand, was gentle and friendly with a warm and rich voice: he did not know cats, having been deprived of their company in childhood, but seemed genuinely interested in what Aristotle had to say. When she rubbed against his legs, he stood still and bent down to gingerly pat her head: never mind that he patted her as he would a dog: she was convinced that in time he could learn the far more complex and sensuous language of cats.

As she dozed off in the comfort of the dictionary, she outlined her campaign to assist Partner make the right choice of their eventual housemate. She sighed softly as she resigned herself to assuming yet another dimension to her job: as though it were not trying enough as it was. Almost immediately she entered the dream she had chosen for today: from one of her earlier lives – perhaps the first as a cat – she surrounded her sleep with memories.

The fourth century before the Christian era was, in her opinion, one of the most damaging to intellectual development: not only for the higher Feline intellect but for all, including the less sophisticated canine, plant, human, bovine and other such intellects. Greek philosophers – most notably her namesake (she never understood why she was thus named, being gender-disparate) – promulgated the superiority of deductive reasoning and the inferiority of inductive: thus the unfortunate, swift, and destructive demise of intuitionalism. Experimentalism reigned supreme ever since, while the natural gift of intuition became so discredited as to be consciously denied as valuable. Intuitive knowledge became an oxymoron: intuitive truth disrespected, disregarded, distrusted, and discarded.

As an alley cat, she never personally knew any philosophers of note: she barely knew any humans, and those she did she preferred not to recall. (Even now, almost 2,500 years later, she mourned the loss of her first litter of kittens – six there were – to the cruelty of three human children.) Many of her friends and acquaintances, however, were house or temple cats and were daily exposed to humans and their bizarre thoughts and behaviors. It was from them she learned of the disturbing trend toward deifying deductive over inductive reasoning and experiment over intuition. Never again would they hold an equal position to properly balance the quest for knowledge and truth.

She dreamed of encountering Partner in a back street of a small village on Crete. Partner was very old, dirty, and clothed in rags: she was clutching a small child in her arms. The child was scrawny with oozing sores on his face, arms, and legs. He whimpered with the weak mew of a starving kitten as flies supped on the pus of his ulcerated skin. Despite the putrid and overwhelming stench that pervaded the scene, Partner maintained her sweet identifying scent of gardenias. Aristotle called and called, but Partner did not recognize her as all her attention was focused on begging alms from the passing marketplace crowds.

As Aristotle watched from the safety of an overturned donkey cart where she had been chatting with the donkey – an old and dear friend – she saw Partner approach Daedalus who was heading for a meeting with King Minos. Suddenly the baby sprouted wings and became Icarus. "What are you doing with my son," shouted Daedalus? Partner was very frightened and was about to run when Aristotle intervened and was able to convince Daedalus that Partner had, in fact, saved Icarus from his fate at the hands of the sun and was bringing him home to Daedalus. Daedalus was so grateful for Partner's kindness, he gave her the wings he was carrying in a large, purple basket. Without a glance at Aristotle, Partner flew straight and true toward a flock of birds that were circling and screeching above.

When Aristotle awakened, it was past noon. The sun had moved from the dictionary to the colorful Turkish prayer rug in the middle of the floor. She remained still with eyes closed as she recalled her dream: what could it mean? No dream was without some purpose; some oblique message. Perhaps this one would become clear after she had a wee nibble of lunch. She stretched, yawned widely, and sauntered toward the kitchen.

Partner had left a tablespoon of soft nibbles in her clean bowl: not quite a lunch, more an afternoon snack: just enough to get her through to dinner. She delicately selected one nibble at a time and thoughtfully – Zen like – experienced her snack. She tried to concentrate on the present, but her thoughts were pulled to the problem that faced her: guiding Partner toward an appropriate choice of mate.

The afternoon passed quietly: between two quick and dreamless catnaps, she completed her usual parole of the premises assuring everything was in order. She spent longer than usual sitting in the front room window, part of her job description, to alert any outsiders that, indeed, the house was well watched over.

Aristotle took pride in her job performance and her contribution to the safety and ambiance of their well-run home. It was not easy attending to all her duties, from maintaining Partner's emotional equilibrium to alerting her to an unlocked door or the timeliness of their meals; graciously greeting every guest to waking Partner each morning regardless of how much she, herself, would like to sleep in. She loved her home and her domestic responsibilities, but there were times when she felt overwhelmed by the demands of keeping up her end of the domestic partnership. She felt tired just thinking about what lay ahead.

It was just after five when she heard Partner's key in the lock. Jumping down from the top of the refrigerator where she was enjoying the hum and warmth of the motor she welcomed her home with the usual enthusiasm. Their reunions, no matter how brief the separation, were always joyous. They missed each other during the workday and felt complete and happy when together.

Partner began her usual homecoming chatter the minute she walked in the door as Aristotle meowed her greeting while entwining herself in Partner's legs. Frequently Partner would plunk herself on the floor to play; today she picked her up and cradled her in her arms while scratching her belly. Aristotle loved to be held in this manner and purred her appreciation, her cobalt ultramarine eyes adoringly regarding the face she knew so well.

"Well, Precious Girl, did you miss me today? Did you eat all your snack? Oh, you must be hungry? Let's see what's for din-din." She snuggled Aristotle close for a minute before putting her on the kitchen counter. Aristotle knew not to jump on the counter when they had company – particularly Partner's parents; apparently others frowned on such freedom in the kitchen.

Reaching into the refrigerator with one hand while scratching Aristotle's chin with the other, Partner continued: "You don't mind eating a bit early today, do you Sweet Angel? It's our turn for the book group tonight, and I want to get ready."

At once disappointed not to be eating with Partner while delighted tonight would offer an opportunity to launch her campaign, Aristotle registered no objections to eating early and alone.

The doorbell rang while she was engaged in her post-dinner ablutions. Giving one last lick to her tail, she hurried into the bedroom to make sure Partner had heard the bell. "They're here," she meowed. "Are you ready?"

"I'm coming, Baby Girl." She scooped her up; holding her under her right arm, she closed the bedroom door with the other. "This will be Suzanne and Wendell. They're always the first to arrive. Does the table look nice? Hope they remembered the wine." She carried her to the front door, placing her on the floor only after opening the door and greeting Suzanne and Wendell.

Aristotle liked both Suzanne and Wendell: they were friendly without being intrusive, good conversationalists without being monopolistic. She greeted them with a warm purr and ankle cuddle. Wendell stooped down to greet her and gently pulled the length of her tail. She meowed softly and turned to offer her tail for an additional tug.

As the other guests arrived; singly, by pairs, and in threes, they received her customary, warm feline welcome with slight variations. She knew each of them from years of such greetings.

Bob arrived with Savita and Rasheesh Singh. Aristotle particularly liked Savita: she spoke a scent that was unlike any other with which she was familiar: richly sweet, dusky and mysterious. Ordinarily she would have focused her attentions on Savita with the expectation of being gently lifted onto her shoulder where she would become lost in the sensuousness of her perfume. Tonight, however, she would forgo this pleasure for the sake of Partner's future happiness.

With obvious delight at the unexpected sedulity of feline attention, Bob, once seated, scooped Aristotle into his lap. "Well girl, you're in fine feline fettle tonight. Are you going to keep me company?"

Aristotle purred and snuggled against Bob's chest. When she saw Partner approach with a tray of hors d'oeuvres, she made a display of her affection for this gentle, witty man.

"My, my," Partner smiled. "She certainly has taken to you tonight. She doesn't usually take to men with such obvious delight. Oh, excuse me." The doorbell had signaled the arrival of her last guest, Reggie.

Reggie's booming voice made Aristotle cringe. Ordinarily she would simply quietly slip out of the room and spend a quiet evening alone in the bedroom, but tonight she had a mission – a most important mission.

As Bob stood to shake Reggie's hand, he gently and respectfully lifted Aristotle to the floor. "Nice to see you, Ol' Boy." He smiled as he took Reggie's hand.

"Hey, Bob. I didn't expect to see you here tonight." Reggie's handshake was aggressively firm with a delayed release just enough to make it clear he thought he was in control. "Hi, all." He gave a wide swoop of his arm in a mock salute to the others in the room as he stooped down to give a casual pat on Aristotle's head.

This was the moment. She felt her heart race and could easily have relinquished her resolve had she not caught a glimpse of beloved Partner. She could not let Partner down.

"Grrrmeow! Hisssssstts!" It was the loudest she had ever spoken, and the ferocity of her outcry startled not only Partner and her guests, but herself as well. She flattened her ears against her head, arched her back, and let out another fearful hiss directed solely at Reggie.

"Jesus Christ!" Reggie jumped back while he instinctively kicked at Aristotle. "What the hell's wrong with that cat? Get outta here!" He kicked again, embarrassed now by his fright and awkward position.

In the ensuing confusion, Aristotle found herself in the protective arms of Bob. That part she had not planned, but it could not have been a better out-come. Partner, startled by the confusion and Aristotle's unexpected behavior, reached to take her from Bob. "Oh, Reggie. I'm so sorry. I don't know what got into her. Here, Bob. I'll take her."

"That's okay," Bob gently stroked Aristotle and headed toward the bedroom. "I'll settle her down in the next room." He assured Partner with a smile and moved toward the bedroom."

"God damned cat." Reggie muttered to no one in particular.

The door closed behind them, Aristotle relaxed in Bob's arms and began to purr loudly. She rubbed her head against Bob's shoulder and felt his gentleness as he lowered her onto the bed. "You don't like him any more than I do, do you girl?" Bob spoke softly and scratched her under the chin. "You better stay in here the rest of the evening."

It was well past midnight when she heard Partner come into the room. Switching on the overhead light, Aristotle squinted and stretched a greeting.

"Well, girl. What was that all about? You never told me before you disliked Reggie so much." She undressed, slipped into her pajamas and crawled into bed beside Aristotle. Yawning, she reached over to turn out the light. "You sure brought out the worst in him." She chuckled as Aristotle snuggled against the inside of her knees.

Emily

She strolled the orchards, hills, and *Lilac Seas** of Amherst. Summer nights and winter dawns – *she started early; took her dog* – witnessed her graceful white and flowing form stepping – stepping light on village lanes and garden paths. No Southern Belle was she; but Belle she be.

> *Soto! Explore thyself!*
> *Therein thyself shalt find*
> *The Undiscovered Continent–*
> *No Settler had in Mind.*

A waif-esque Settler, she explored the undiscovered continent yet, nowhere in that fertile mind – that soft, green *Alabaster Chamber* of luminescent light – did she envisage the fame she consciously sought.

Barely 32, she answered a call for new poets in the local press. In her careful and very small script – *small like a sparrow* – she addressed the envelope bearing the letter that would change the life of both the writer and the recipient:

To Thomas Wentworth Higgins, Worcester, Massachusetts:

Dear Sir:

> *I smile when you suggest I delay "to publish" – that being*
> *Foreign to me as Firmament to Fin.*
> *If Fame belongs to me, I could not escape her – if she did not,*
> *The longest day would pass me on the chase – and the approbation*
> *Of my Dog would forsake me – then – My Barefoot-Rank is better.*
> *You think my gait "spasmodic." I am in danger, Sir.*
> *You think me "uncontrolled." I have no tribunal . . .*
> *The Sailor cannot see the North, but knows the Needle can.*

Fame. That elusive *Currency of Immortality*. That cold and calculating *Auction Of the Mind of Man* possessed her spirit until, at thirty-two, she finally resigned herself to her destiny – a poet who in her 55 years of life would remain unknown.

Resignation. Yet the *White Heat* of her creativity soundlessly tugged within her maiden breast. Her pen – always a pen – pumped nurturing blood into the crimson veins of her thoughts and birthed them on paper. Infants alive with holy helium that brooked no tether. Round and robust children floating up and ever up toward Awe. Like a cat she greedily lapped the after-birth and felt it nourish her and reproduce again and again from the same life-giving blood.

She determined to remain no *Beggar at the Door for Fame* and thus – virginal mother she – birthed ever more babies to populate her World of Beauty. Her Universe of Love.

And walking this Sunday dawn – in her vestal white dress that defines her identity – she looks to the horizon and measures the time when villagers would awaken and threaten her solitude. She hurries homeward to her narrow room which is wider, fuller, and higher than the church to which her neighbors speed to congregate and pray to their Christian God – the same God she has successfully dispatched along with the brightly colored dresses that thrill the vestibule. Atheist she may be judged by those who whisper of her eccentricities. While they find *A God* in their Sunday building, she entertains many gods in her term spent between birth and death. If they *knew,* if they were capable of *knowing,* they would envy her Developed Spirit.

>*Behind Me – dips Eternity –*
>*Before Me – Immortality –*
>*Myself – the Term between –*

Alone now in the mellifluous aura of her humble cathedral – that narrow room the width of oceans – she holds pen in hand as she gazes from her window across to her neighbors' home. The Evergreens, where her brother Austin lives (alas, unfaithfully) with her sister-in-law, Susan. Beautiful Susan: Her Pearl. Her Gem. Her Muse. Her beloved Passion. Brilliant and cold as a diamond. The thought of Susan created in our haunted and holy mystic, our poet, *a tighter breathing and Zero at the bone.*

Her posture, a quiet dignity in her straight-backed chair, matches the quiet dignity of her poetry but belies the humid warmth of her uterus and thunderous cacophony of her heartbeat as she writes:

>One Life *of so much Consequence!*
>*Yet I – for it – would pay –*
>*My Soul's* entire income –
>*In ceaseless – salary –*
>
>One Pearl – *to me – so signal –*
>*That I would instant dive –*
>*Although – I* knew *– to* take *it –*

Would cost me – just a life!
The Sea is full – I know it!
That – does not blur my Gem!
It burns – distinct from all the row –
Intact – in Diadem!

The life is thick – I know it!
Yet – not so dense a crowd –
But Monarchs – are perceptible –
Far down the dustiest Road!

The house is quiet with all at church. No longer does the family comment on her discarding of church observance – or her discarding of all social interactions, for that matter. She worships at the alter of Love, Nature, Eternity, and Immortality. Her prayer is Language in all its possibilities. She muses about Kierkegaard: *If he is right and religion is a poetry of fixed metaphors, does that make her poetry an untethered religion? Free of man-made churches, priests, and superstitions?* She answers her own question with a resounding and joyous *yes!* Her heightened spiritual state is not disputed by any who know her. Not even the most judgmental of her non-Christ-like Christian neighbors who gossiped about her blazing her own theological trails. Their gossip – the talk of small minds – would sadden Jesus of Nazareth were he to eavesdrop. Christians indeed!

As for her increasingly anti-social seclusion and reclusive withdrawal to that narrow birthing room of poems: she refused to allow mundane social conventions to diminish her contemplative monastic (convent sans convention?) life. She was strong enough to defy the Victorian patriarchy and replace it with her own female language and values. *I may live in the Victorian time in history,* she thought, *but I am most certainly not a Victorian womyn.*

Church service would soon be out and the family would return for their joyous Sunday meal. She left her cathedral and descended to the kitchen to prepare a meal for their return. There would be visitors following dinner – as there was every Sunday. And, as always, she would sequester herself in her room for the duration of their stay. Depending on who dropped by, she might quietly creep to the top of the stairs to listen (eavesdrop) to their conversations. But never – *never* – would she join them.

Sunday dinner over and the dining room and kitchen shining, the guests began arriving. Voices drifted up the stairs and under the low wooden door of her sanctuary. *The tea is lovely dear. Wasn't Pastor Thomas's sermon moving today? Did you notice that Sarah's husband wasn't in attendance today? Tsk! Tsk!* None piqued her interest until a high-pitched and highly excitable female voice pierced her consciousness. Mrs. Samuel Bowles – wife of the scandalously worldly editor of the *Springfield Republican* was regaling the company with her plans for a trip to Boston.

Emily quietly settled herself on the top stair and listened. If she could not hear his voice – her Master, her Protector, her Sun, her Earl – she would settle for the grating voice of his wife.

Four o'clock and tea is done. Guests are homeward bound, and the warm sun is embracing her as she sits yet again with her pen, passions, and her elegant posture in that straight-backed chair:

Wild Nights – Wild Nights!
Were I with thee
Wild Nights should be
Our luxury!

Futile – the Winds –
To a heart in port –
Done with the Compass –
Done with the Chart!

Rowing in Eden –
Ah, The Sea!
Might I but moor – Tonight –
In Thee!

She moored each night in that narrow room that held the Universe and her passions. Alone. One thousand seven hundred seventy-five babies birthed and folded and tucked away for future fame. Fame she nor they imagined.

Her death was meant to be in the spring. When eternal life returns singing promises of an earthly heaven and the continuation of the Developed Spirit. Flowers sing hallelujahs to the immortality of Life. She had successfully burned away – in a transfiguration of spirit into art – the hells of this earth: oppression, ignorance, eroticism, nationality, religiosity, gender, race, age, and materialism. All that was left was the Blaze of the Developed Spirit: *Without a Color, but the light /Of unanointed Blaze.*

>May 15, 1886 she
>*Dropped into the Ether Acre –*
>*Wearing the Sod Gown –*
>*Bonnet of Everlasting Laces –*
>*Brooch – frozen on –*
>*Horses of Blonde – and Coach of Silver –*
>*Baggage a strapped Pearl –*
>*Journey of Down – and Whip of Diamond –*
>*Riding to meet the Earl –*

---

* Words, lines, and complete poems of Emily Dickinson are listed in order of their appearance and are identified by the number system of Thomas H. Johnson's *The Complete Poems of Emily Dickinson:* #1337, #520, #832, #216, #406, #709, #365, #1240, #721, #986, #270, #249, #365, #665.

Maria

She walked intentionally toward the gate counter behind which stood a bored, lusterless flight attendant. The attendant, pecking at a keyboard on the counter, did not look up although surely she was aware of a passenger standing before her. Maria waited patiently, making neither movement nor sound to signal irritation.

The gate – number 38 – was at the end of a long tunnel served by a moving walkway. For the sake of exercise – of which she got little – she had forgone the walkway in favor of walking. The walk felt good but left her somewhat breathless, flushed, and damp.

She placed her two bags on the floor, one on either side of her. She prided herself on traveling light; rarely taking more luggage than she could carry on board. The two bags held all she would need to see her comfortably through her four days in DC: clothes, two books – the last half of Lawrence Darrell's *Alexandria Quartet,* her lap-top, toiletries, and, of course, her faithful traveling companion, Saint Christopher Bear: she'd place him on her hotel bed as soon as she unpacked. He was her travel totem. Her silent companion of the road, air, and seas. As his namesake carried the Babe across the raging river, so too did this Saint Christopher carry her safely to her destinations and home again.

From her jacket pocket she withdrew a pen and small pad of paper on which she wrote a brief note. The attendant could not ignore her forever. Again she resumed her mute and motionless posture before the counter. It became a curious game as to how long the attendant could (would) pretend she was unaware of her presence.

Half a minute. A minute. A minute and a half. She was disappointed when a rather rakish looking gray-haired traveler with a laptop in one hand and a paper cup of coffee in the other approached the counter. She had wanted to play out the hand between herself and the attendant.

"Excuse me," he said, "is this the flight to Washington?"

Self-importantly, the attendant made two last stabs at the keyboard and looked up with an overplayed expression of surprise that was meant to convey, *Oh, my! I didn't realize someone was waiting for my invaluable assistance.*

"Is this the flight to DC?" he repeated.

The condescension in the attendant's smile was lost on the harried businessman. Without looking at the board behind her, she pointed to the clearly marked sign: *Washington, DC – Flight #65019.*

"Thanks," he said as he distractedly moved off toward one of the plastic bucket seats in the waiting area.

Having dispensed with one irritant, she turned to Maria. Without the courtesy of a *"May I help you?"* or even a curt *"Yes?"* she raised her perfectly shaped eyebrows and ever-so-slightly cocked her head to make the inquiry for her.

Maria let her most winsome smile play over her face as she gently pushed the note forward along with her ticket. *What an insignificant, self-deluded jerk,* she thought. *She truly believes her position as clerk/waitress for the airlines places her above her customers. Does everyone turning to her for guidance convince her of her elevated status?*

Upon reading the note – "I was told you could issue my boarding pass here. May I be assigned to an isle seat?" – the attendant's supercilious attitude melted to be replaced by a cloying, fawning attention. While checking the computer for available seats and preparing the boarding pass, she graced Maria with the unnatural and chilling smile of the egoist. "I WILL CALL YOU WHEN IT IS TIME." Her mouth exaggerated the words, and her voice was that of a robot with the volume on high.

"Oh, dear," she muttered to herself. Taking the pen from Maria's hand, she jotted on the pad "I will come and get you when it is time to board."

Maria, smiling, nodded and gestured with her right hand what she thought might be understood as American Sign for "Thank you."

As she moved toward the plastic chairs the attendant, with a flourish of what she thought passed for compassionate aide, hustled out from behind her hiding place to usher Maria to the nearest seat. *I'm deaf, not feeble* she wanted to shout as she again smiled and signed her version of "Thank you."

The businessman, now seated comfortably and casually observing the interaction, smiled at Maria as she settled into the wait. *Would he smile at me if he didn't know I was deaf,* she wondered. She acknowledged his smile with an ever-so-slight movement of her head; so slight it could not be categorized as a nod.

Glancing at her boarding pass, she noticed for the first time her seat number: 13-C and wondered at the significance.

The chaos and cacophony of the waiting area increased as departure time neared. She closed her eyes and concentrated on becoming invisible: deaf and blind to the babble and rush that swirled around her: to swim out of the whirling torrent of travelers not up but down. Down into the depths of quiet. Down into the serenity of lightlessness. Down into floating, airless solitude.

Gradually the desperately coveted deafness embraced her. She was, at last, fully within herself: free from the jarring jumble. The physicality of people and things. The drowning whirlpool of connectedness. As she entered deafness, she invariably thought of Hamlet's last words: *The rest is silence.* She smiled.

There was less than ten minutes before she would be boarded. She knew she should have waited until she was settled on board before entering her deafness. But it had been so long – too long – since last she had the opportunity. She prayed she would be able to resume occupancy of that cool and dark domain after boarding.

A light touch on her arm. The gate attendant was saying something. Maria lingered in her deafness for one final moment before opening her eyes. The waiting room was abuzz with activity. A harried mother attempting to juggle her infant in one arm while gathering a diaper bag, her purse, and a small carry-on piece in the other, all the while instructing her toddler to hold onto her skirt and hurry. "Hurry!" The infant, crying now, dropped (threw?) her bottle. It rolled under the row of plastic seats. A slight groan from the mother as she gently shoved the boy toward the bottle. "Joshua, please get the bottle for Mommy. Hurry!" Joshua, now suddenly shy and clinging to Mommy's skirt, hung his head and moved closer to Mommy's legs.

"Joshua, please," her voice was sharp and exasperated. Joshua began whining and clung more tenaciously to Mommy's legs.

The gray haired businessman was closing up his laptop in preparation for being called to board. His empty coffee container was on the floor by his feet. He glanced at Mommy and, spying the bottle under the seat of a long-legged, lounging back-packer, he stood and placed his computer on his seat.

"Excuse me." The lounging back-packer, legs stretched into the narrow aisle between seats, was oblivious to the bottle and the challenge his extended personal territory posed to pedestrian traffic. "Excuse me," the businessman repeated as he indicated to the back-packer the bottle under his seat.

Obviously annoyed, Backpacker slowly – ever so slowly – gathered his nearly horizontal body into the chair and moved ever so slightly to the right allowing Businessman to reach under the seat to retrieve the bottle.

Gate Attendant tapped Maria's arm again, attempting to get her attention. "YOU CAN BOARD NOW." The volume of the robot was again on high, and her exaggerated mouthing of the words was, if anything, more pronounced. The irritation she had originally felt for Gate Attendant was replaced by resignation. "Thank you", she signed with a smile. Gathering her two bags, she obediently followed Gate Attendant to the podium where another attendant awaited to receive her boarding pass.

"This one is deaf," she informed her colleague. Then, to Maria, "HAVE A NICE TRIP." Maria accepted her portion of the boarding pass and proceeded into the tunneled walkway.

In front of her Mommy, Joshua, and Baby Sister struggled down the tunnel toward the gaping maw of the plane. Joshua began screaming for Mommy to carry him, also. Though she had a firm grip of his small wrist, he refused to remain at her side and twisted to position himself in front of her forcing her to stop and yank him back to her side. The diaper bag and purse had slid from her shoulder and were hanging from her crooked left arm that held the baby. Both were dragging on the floor despite Mommy's twitches and contortions attempting to raise her overburdened arm.

Maria quickened her step to bring her directly behind the trio. She touched Mommy's shoulder causing her to jump and turn toward her. Maria was startled by her face which was filled with such depths of terror from the gentle but unexpected touch that Maria gasped. Their eyes held each other for the briefest of moments and slowly the terror receded: without a word Maria took Mommy's diaper bag and purse. She shifted her own baggage to accommodate the two new burdens. She smiled to herself as she thought, *No matter how much baggage we insist on hauling around, we can always make room for more.*

The trio – now a quartet – advanced toward the entrance to the plane. Joshua, intrigued by the addition to their little party, was suddenly subdued and walked quietly beside Mommy. No one made a sound, even Baby Sister was silent as her huge, luminous eyes soberly observed the newcomer.

Maria stood quietly blocking the aisle while Mommy settled her wee family in their seats. Backpacker was now impatiently huffing behind her. His audible irritation at her blocking the isle for the convenience of Mommy and children brought a smile to Maria's face and encouraged her to linger ever-so-slightly longer than necessary. Baby Sister on her lap and Joshua strapped into the seat beside her, Mommy smiled up at Maria. Silently Maria placed the diaper bag and purse on the floor between Mommy's feet.

About to move on down the aisle to 13-C, their eyes again engaged in that ancient silent communion between (and among) womyn who *know*. For a moment Maria was tempted to sit in the empty seat across the isle. But why? What could she say or do to ease the pain of this young mother. She could say no more than her eyes had already relayed: *We are sisters. I acknowledge your strength. Travel light. Share your knowing and strength with Joshua and Baby Sister.*

Maria saw them once more – fleetingly – as she stepped of the curb into the waiting taxi. They were again three, but now appeared to be One. Baby Sister was happily settled in an umbrella stroller that Joshua gently, earnestly, and self-importantly pushed along the sidewalk beside Mommy.

"Joshua," Maria shouted. It was the first word she had uttered since entering her deafness in the airport. All three turned toward her as she smiled and waved. In unison they returned her wave and smile. As her taxi jolted from the curb she was warmed by the serenity of Mommy's face.

Elefantina

She hummed softly – almost imperceptibly – as a gentle smile played across her full mouth turning her round, kind face into a study of serenity. Through the dense forest canopy she could glimpse the progress of the full moon inching toward dawn and the completion of the nocturnal work of each.

The yet unanswered question tickled her with every full moon: on the eastern horizon He appears large and orange but pales in size and color as He rises, arches, and descends in the west. The mystery of this phenomenon of perception continues to challenge minds too limited by the restrictions of science to comprehend, but she understood from the knowledge of her heart's purity: Luna Time was slow time providing her with eons of swirling, brilliant seconds, minutes, and ages to put to eternal rest her task at hand.

The forest floor, spongy with thousands of years of fertile foliage fallen and absorbed into earth, yielded easily to her spade. Just as she delicately selected minute bits of food from her English bone china dinner plate (Ansley Black Imperial) onto her sterling silver fork (International Fern Spray) when she dined, so too she delicately lifted minute bits of earth onto the tip of her spade as she created the sacred sacrificial hole on the edge of the forest.

She had come out from England with her missionary parents when only a girl. The bustling seaport village overwhelmed her with its cacophony of traffic: ships, sailors, cows, bicycles, water-buffalo carts, monkeys, beggars, fish mongers, prostitutes, children, dogs, wild parrots, baggage carriers, money changers, and men from every corner of the earth. She was relieved when her parents chose to build their small cottage on the far side of the village in a clearing at the edge of the forest. The sounds and stench of the city did not penetrate their tiny bit of paradise.

Now, over seventy years later, it is in that very same cottage she continues to live and carry on her mission; somewhat different from the mission of her parents but none-the-less important. The village grew and grew into what was now a full-fledged town, (the railroad came in the 1940's). Blessedly it sprawled its ever-increasing height and density along the edge of the sea and did not intrude on the serenity of her clearing that clung to the tails of her forest primeval.

The cottage, like her, was small, cozy, and comfortable exuding the warmth and presence that glowed from a Thomas Kinkaid print. The parlor and dining room on the first floor were always embraced by the aroma of home, the home in which so many of her borders who came and went from the three bedrooms on the second floor wished they had grown up.

The dining room, with its long and sturdy table and matching sideboard, was witness to thousands of meals over the years. As a child she fondly recalled Mother serving breakfast to her and Father exactly at 6:15 each morning and dinner at precisely 6:15 each evening. She and Father took lunch pails to school and work respectively, and mother's lunch was a mystery. The 6:15 dining tradition remained with only the server and diners changing. Now it was she instead of Mother serving and the diners were an ever-changing array of borders from across the globe. And, as Mother's custom, every meal was preceded by Grace: "Bless this food and bless this home and thank you God for providing both." The gentle, homey refinement of her dining room never made necessary a reminder to her borders that coarse language was not welcomed. Such language simply never found its way into her cottage.

The parlor's overstuffed chairs with dainty doilies on the arms and head rest were warm and welcoming for her travel weary borders who quietly read or played checkers or enjoyed the conversation of fellow borders of an evening following their hearty and always delicious dinner.

The heart of the cottage was her kitchen, and she slept in the main artery of that heart, a small pantry she had converted into her cell. She had never actually seen a convent cell but envisioned it to be sparse, clean, and strictly utilitarian. Jesus hung on a simple crucifix above her bed and watched over her pretty and gentle dreams as she drifted through them each night.

The moon washed over her as she continued to dig. Over the years she had dug more than 400 such sacred holes, 417 to be exact. And she was nothing if not exact. She maintained a careful, neat ledger of the particulars of each sacrifice: date, weather, precise location of hole, description of her offering, menu of last meal, and precise quote of final words.

The holes did not have to be deep; no more than three feet, and she paced her patient excavations so she was invigorated rather than tired by the time the moon set and the last spade full of rich forest loam was lovingly spread and patted on the now refilled sacred hole.

Her work was slow and steady – as the natives say, "The only way to eat an elephant is one bite at a time" – while her moon-shadow crept from behind her to in front of her so that by the time she was replacing the final blanket of earth on her sacrifice, her shadow rested on the slight mound as a blessing for her moonlit enterprise.

Dawn found her back in her tidy kitchen preparing her famous veggie omelets, mango chutney, bread hot from her oven, freshly churned butter, fresh squeezed juice, and tea, which she served – with shy pride – to her remaining borders; those not fortunate enough to be chosen for her communion offering. (The Lamb of God taketh away the sins of the world . . . but, the Lamb must be pure.)

Actually, it was not the final nocturnal disposition that was the most difficult phase of her work; far more challenging was the arduous effort expended in selecting the offering. She was, however, put on this earth with a sacred mission, and she most diligently fulfilled it without complaint (not even in her heart), fatigue, or question.

Just as God sent his beloved son to Earth to be brutally sacrificed on Calvary for the sins of man, so, too, she was sent to Earth to select additional worthy lambs (although, surely, none could be found as worthy as the original, but she did her humble best to come as close as worldly men could achieve). God did his part by sending them to her door. It was up to her to do her part by selecting the most worthy.

In the early years they came only twice a month when the ships arrived from the north and anchored in the bay. The commerce increased as the port became known for its relaxed business practices and friendly natives. Ships began arriving more and more frequently so that single men, seeking a bed and hot meal, became so plentiful she rarely saw a week she was not forced to turn some away. (No room at the inn.)

Salesmen, scholars, sailors; Scottish, Turkish, Chinese; young, old, rich, poor – they were directed to the small cottage just outside town in the fragrantly gardened clearing a hair's breadth (or is it a hare's breath?) from the rich and rainy forest. Despite her years of experience, she could not tell from first impressions which ones would be worthy. Sometimes those that, on first impression, appeared promising turned out to be the least while those who first appeared unlikely were ultimately the winners.

Her pre-qualifying test was simple, consisting only of three parts: speech, deportment, and hygiene. Often a stevedore would appear at her gate unshaven, disheveled, and dirty. Rather than turn him away she learned to wait until dinner to see what he made of himself once ushered to his room and bath. On the other hand, a traveling salesman may appear tidy, slick, and perfumed but at dinner his true character would be revealed in his uncouth manners or uninformed and unrefined speech.

Regardless of their being disqualified from consideration as offerings, she was, nonetheless, gracious and hospitable throughout their stay. Most stayed only two or three days while they completed their business and sailed with the next departing ship. Some were regulars who came through once a month or two or three times a year and always received a warm welcome.

Tonight's offering was a particularly splendid one, and her humming was the purr of contentment that infuses the soul of those who love their work and know they've achieved a singular perfection of accomplishment.

He lay immobile on the clean pink and yellow quilt where she had instructed him to wait while she worked. The forest tea she served him after dinner worked its magic as always: by the time she cleared the table, washed and dried the dishes, and re-set the table for the morning's omelets, he was sitting silent and calm in his room ready to follow her quiet directions. He bathed, perfumed, dressed in clean clothes, packed his valise and followed her through the moon-lit garden to the chosen site where she had spread the quilt. She spoke softly so as not to alarm him; fear would produce a body odor that would diminish the quality of her offering and result in fewer sins of man being redeemed.

He gazed at her uncomprehendingly but with trust in her gentle wisdom. As the moon swam through the golden moonriver toward the west, she removed the last bit of earth and was prepared to lovingly roll him from the quilt to the holy hole. His eyes were closed and his breathing shallow. As she lifted the far edge of the quilt and pulled it over him and toward the hole, he rolled effortlessly into place. He was face down and she bent to turn his head so he could breath and placed his valise under his cheek. His eyes fluttered open, and they smiled into hers before closing again.

It took her less than ten minutes to replace the dirt over him and pat the slight mound smooth.

When the lodgers made their way down to breakfast they found her efficiently squeezing papaya juice. The warm aroma of fresh baked bread and veggie omelets greeted them, and the gaily flowered pink and yellow quilt, freshly laundered, was a homey flag on the clothes line in the clearing.

Consummation

They were now so long together, they lost the edge of the sea and shore between them and floated on the calm tide that flowed unimpeded from her arteries to his and back and forth as in eternity.

The waves of their lives merged – indistinguishable – and cleansed from their shared soul and memory the past savageries and putrid odors.

One thing only remained to fully consummate their centuries old marriage. "I will not die until we succeed," she told him each night as they tenderly tucked each other into bed. And him – for his part – pleaded with his subconscious to cooperate.

From the beginning of their time together, she invited their dreams to follow them from the depths of darkest sleep into the golden lightness of dawn and beyond. Throughout the centuries and the universe, breakfast communions between lovers evolves into habits – revealing habits – disclosing the most subtle personalities of relationships: the schedule of the day ahead; the previous night's lovemaking – or the sullen sadness of the lack-thereof; the revelation's of the morning newspaper; the weather; or – the worst of all – silence. Observe the couple's morning routines, and you see the skeleton and soul of the marriage.

For them, as they performed their early morning ablutions, they each silently reviewed their dreams: those nocturnal friends who weave our past and future into a fabric of colorful desire. "You're judged by the company you keep."

Teeth brushed, skin sudsed, chin shaved, excretions flushed, and hair arranged, they silently prepare to break their fast. He measures three tablespoons of coffee into the fluted white filter of the coffee maker. She crosses behind him to take the prune juice from the ice box and fills the two ancient juice glasses – the only two remaining from the set his mother gave them for their wedding centuries past. He places the English muffins in the toaster. She takes the eggs and sausage from the ice box and breaks the eggs in one fry pan while he turns the sausage in the other. Silently they stand side by side at the range – their bodies magnetically – thaumaturgically – seeking the whisper of contact that touches the depths of their calm and aqua souls.

The breakfast table – set by him the previous eve while she put away the dinner dishes – sparkles in the sun that streams through the eastern window. Their chairs – not at either end of the table – rather side-by-side facing across the table and out the window – are worn and shiny from eons of rumps seeking the solace of breaking fasts and bread together in the light of new days.

Looking at each other with a palpable yearning hope that this will be the morning their beings are at last entwined in an eternal embrace, they divulge their dreams of the previous night.

Every breakfast shared over the centuries of their togetherness – in all that time they have never spent a night or a breakfast apart – the hope is as high as ever it was in the beginning as blushing bride and groom. Their bodies united. Their souls united. Their spirits united. Surely no two beings could be as one without that final and most intimate of unions – their dreams – also reaching toward each other and metamorphosing into one.

Soon. Very soon. They were sure. The diaphanous diaphragm separating them from their physical life was becoming more and more fragile.

Without preliminaries he began: "A gaggle of geese – very ordinary geese – chased me across a large and well-kept farm yard."

"I was chased by no geese," she replied sadly. Resignedly.

"But wait," he offered hopefully, "There's more. A wave came – a tsunami but benevolent. All 200,000 Indonesians that went with the 2005 tsunami returned. They were laughing and dancing and dry as talcum. 'We were only at the One Hundred Year Festival' they explained. They were perplexed by the interest in and fear of their return."

He embraced her as she lowered her head onto her arms. "No tsunami," she whispered. "Perhaps tonight the gossamer film between our dreams will rent and allow them to embrace, entwine, and at last be one."

He held her until her Hope regained energy, and she lifted her head and washed him with the darkly disturbing light of her old eyes.

Every breakfast of their 74 years together, those eyes had offered him their cleansing benediction that stretched back into the Earth deeply penetrating the surface strata to the core of molten lava. They were the color of zapote – that sweet and sensuous Mexican chocolate fruit – with deep green rims thinly circling the darkest of black chocolate irises. And like zapote they never failed to leave a sensuous and sweet aftertaste.

She washed the breakfast dishes as he set their window-hugging table for their mid-day meal. Both worked slowly, lingeringly – but not lugubriously – so as to postpone by even a few precious moments the time they would kiss goodbye and separate for those long and lonely hours until noon.

She to her cleaning, cooking, and sock-mending. He to his animal husbandry, mowing, milking, mucking, and fence-mending.

Those hours of separation – agonizingly long for both – were wrapped in the silence of solitude and the aching yearning for their noontime re-union. Those hours of separation suspended their shared soul and mind and spirit, and the colorless winds of loneliness whirled through their beings. Finding no soul, mind, or spirit, the winds entered their arteries, their intestines, their brains leaving them exhausted, frightened, and transformed into plodding mules with only one intent – to earn their right to head home.

And so they melted into their parting kiss that must sustain them until noon. The kiss of the united: bloodless even though the lavender blood of her veins surged into his arteries while the sea-green blood of his veins flowed smoothly from his internal canals into hers.

The octopus hours of their separation swam by in slow, slinky waves of loose-limbed tentacles. Occasionally the raven ink of depression, yearning, and longing sprayed each with its thick and heavy liquor of loneliness. Their perseverance swayed with the octopus dance but never faltered beyond recovery.

Six of the clock. Seven. Eight. The energy of their parting kiss remained palpable. Sweet and sensuous the smell. Nine. Ten. The scent of the kiss weakened, overpowered by the fetid smell of formaldehyde from they knew not where. It wafted around them seeking entry into any orifice willing to admit it: ears, nose, eyes, mouth. Anus. Vagina. Penis. Pores. All must remain vigilant as the acid odor strengthened, as the energy of the kiss waned. Formaldehyde crept into the corners of their bedroom as she smoothed the sheets and fluffed the pillows. Formaldehyde wended its way through the cattle stalls as he mucked the sweet manure of his pretty and gentle Herefords and laid fresh straw.

They braced for the final challenge – the Eleventh Hour struggle – and sloughed, slogged, and slid through their war with formaldehyde.

Smiling fondly at the cows, he gently closed the barn doors and slowly pushed up the slope to their Kinkaid-esque cottage. She watched the tea pot as it came to a boil and finally – finally –

whistled in its daily duet with the distant village church bells tolling twelve.

Their mid-day meal was joyous, hot, and long. Meat. Potatoes. Hot and cold vegetables. Milk. Bread. All from their own handiwork. And desserts over which they lingered with tea and conversation. It was the dessert and conversation only that varied in their routine. And it was the dessert and conversation that filled their afternoon hours before their shared sun-down chores.

Some days they shared zucchini-pecan cake with cream cheese frosting as they discussed their plans for their afterlife. Other days they relished his mother Anna's muffins with walnuts and raisins as they giggled together over memories of their young coming together. Strawberry-rhubarb pies and politics. Chocolate-sour cream cake and philosophy. Cherry cheese cake and their favorite Gabriel Garcia Marquez short story. Carmel-nut ice cream sundaes and news from their Mexican friends in San Miguel de Allende, Guanajuato.

Their dessert and conversation shifted with the sun – from the breakfast table to the dining room table – also snuggled against a window – this time facing west over the rolling hills and the setting sun.

Their spirits rose as the sun descended ever more in the west and their end of day chores – always completed side-by-side – were done, and it was time to ascend the narrow, creaking stairs to their loft where their bed – the bed in which he was born – awaited their dreams.

"I will not die until we succeed," said, as she did each night, as he tucked the corner of their comforter under her left shoulder that she could not reach and she tucked the opposing corner under his right shoulder and under his chin, allowing her thin-skinned and veined hand to caress his cheeks, lips, and eyes.

"Tonight," he replied. "Tonight for sure."

She drifted off quickly – with her sigh of desideration – as she always did; his chest, stomach, loins, and legs coiled against her warm, soft rump, back, and shoulders. The flesh of one indistinguishable from the flesh of the other – indeed eliminating "other" – as they melted together co-joined and comfortable.

He listened for her even breathing before he dared to enter that realm of dreams where his and hers would embrace as one – as they had for decades. And, in that brief twilight of time between her words and her sleeping breath, he conjured the "dream" he would share with her at breakfast.

Olive

She would have been the baby of the family even if she were not the last born. Simple-minded and sluggish from birth, Olive slogged through life sans spark, sans energy, sans passion. "Dull as a box of rocks," some in the family quipped.

Her presence – body and spirit – was rectangular as opposed to the circular and square essences of her six sisters and four brothers. The unfortunate geometry of her mind did not allow for free flow of thoughts or the perpetual motion of ideas bouncing off equilateral sides. All that entered her mind sank to the bottom to languish, rot, and eventually expel the putrid odor of decaying flesh unique to the living dead.

The shape of her body mirrored that of her spirit; rectangular with no hint of neck, breasts, waist, buttocks, calves, or ankles. Straight, hard lines unadorned or softened by curves or the hint of indentations.

Like the drupe for which she was named, Olive bore a hard, stony center surrounded by bitter and salty flesh.

The dullness of her body was repeated in the spiritless gaze of her uncomprehending eyes. Their shallow depths precluded the presence of soul and bathed those upon whom her gaze fell with a chill that lingered well after the gaze somnambulantly slithered on to other objects.

While her siblings – circles and squares by turns – pitied the sterile life assigned to their baby sister, they could not imagine any alternative for a rectangular, stone-centered womyn-child.

It was at the exact moment the phone rang that the smell of molten steel wrapped its hard-edged acridity around my neurotransmitters and took up residence in every cell of my body. As I spoke with the womyn at the other end of the line – a line that stretched all the way across the country and into another life – I could hear the smell sizzling through my body. When the womyn identified herself as the director of Aqua Fria Nursing Home in Boston, the molten steel stench plummeted – as if in a fast dropping elevator – from my cerebral cortex to my intestines; and there it stayed as I heard the news that Olive was dying, and she had listed me – *why me?* – on her intake forms as next of kin.

The conversation ended, but the stinging and hot odor of steaming liquid steel remained steadfast in my intestines, and the metallic taste could not be rinsed from my mouth.

It had been 30 or more years since I'd seen – or even heard tell of – Olive. It was perhaps nearly as long since even a thought of her entered my awareness. My cross-country trip to her deathbed was surreal – a slow-motion dream of one's childhood lived underwater. Cold water.

Aqua Fria Nursing Home was located in the squalid bowels of Roxbury. With what wise or wicked humor did the name of this rundown terminal come to be? The geographic jolt of language was all the more jarring in contrast with the oppressive humidity of Boston in July. No heat is more enervating than New England's soggy, suffocating summers. One such day of mildewed and mould infested air is too high a price to pay for the promise of weeks of relief on the shores of the Cape, New Hampshire, or Maine. Cold water, indeed!

While waiting for my eyes to adjust upon entering her darkened room, I sensed their presence but could not quite identify who they were. Slowly iris, retina, and lens re-aligned, converged, and focused in the dim light that wept from the edges of the drapes and slithered under the closed door of what I assumed to be the bathroom.

Propped against pillows, she was more horizontal than vertical while being neither. Her head was turned toward me and if her eyes were open she would see me outlined in the doorway. Silently I closed the door behind me and moved around the foot of the bed to the window. There was neither sound nor movement from the bed but as I reached to gently part the drapes, the icicles of her voice pierced the dim silence, "Don't!"

My gasp was as much from the startle of her voice as from the frigid burning stench that accompanied it. The putrid odor of death wrapped around me, sucked the breath from my body, and pressed me down into the one chair – cushionless, armless, straight-backed, metal – beside her bed.

Silence was gone, replaced not by sound but by smell – a smell that wafted memories and tactile sensations as it overpowered all time, space, and universal consciousness. Eternity stretched between seconds and seconds slipped into minutes awaiting the return of my breath.

Slowly – as Earth moves beneath a plane at high altitude – the Others drifted out of the dimness. Power. Grief. Shadow. From the fathomless depths of the Human Psyche, they revealed their presence. Guilt. Regret. Anger. They crowded the room and drenched the air with a numbing blue sap that coated everything – bed, chair, night stand, dresser, drapes, walls, ceiling, floor – everything in that small room coated with the horror. Hubris. Shame. Hate. They slyly sucked the sap from their external intestines and were nourished and strengthened by the slime.

"You're old." Her voice, though almost a whisper now, remained sharp with icicles and blue with passive cold.

"You're dying." Was my voice as cold and passive as hers? It sounded forced to me as I consciously projected it to what I hoped was my normal conversational volume, refusing to enter the intimacy of a returned whisper.

Throbbing silence. The Others gleefully danced around us swinging the tentacles of their intestines above their heads.

The cacophony of silence clambered throughout the room as the room metamorphosed into the Universe. Nothing existed outside this Hellish space, no escape possible sans death or compassion.

Hours passed. We spoke of many things. Past and present – but never future. Circles and squares – but never rectangles. And as we spoke the Others – lacking nourishment – tucked their intestines inside and – seeking more fertile realms – vaporized and disappeared.

The edges of the drapes were now dark and the only light was from beneath the doors.

"You must go." The icicles – though still there – were less piercing.

"As you, too, must go," I whispered. For the first time since childhood, I touched her. My touch was light and spontaneous. Her parchment covered hand did not respond, but her eyes briefly glowed in the dark, and the tension of her neck relaxed as her head settled ever so slightly into the pillow.

Had the stench really gone with the Others or had my olfactory awareness simply adjusted to it as had my eyes to the dark? In any event, it no longer occupied my awareness as I stepped out of Aqua Fria into the now dark but still drippingly humid Boston night.

Readers' Guide:
Questions for Discussion Groups

Cover Art:

1. In many cultures today, e.g., Jewish, Hindu, Islamic, Jain, Christian, etc. womyn in their monthly flow are forbidden to touch holy books, participate in religious rituals, enter places of worship or even their own kitchen. What cultural and societal developments contribute to the contemporary view of the female genitalia as dirty and shameful?

2. How can we successfully raise our sons and daughters to return due reverence and respect to both female and male genitalia?

Preface:

1. The great American Pulitzer Prize winning author, Willa Cather said "There are only two or three human stories, and they go on repeating themselves as fiercely as if they never happened before." What are those two or three human stories, and how are they represented in this collection of short stories?

2. What does the author mean when she says, "There is no such thing as fiction?"

About the Author:

1. Why did an alternative spelling of woman/women develop and why does the author choose to use the alternative "womyn"?

Pyracantha:

1. Why is Love capitalized as a proper noun?

2. How does the Green Fire differ from red, blue, and white fire?

3. Why are Green Fire and Love incompatible?

4. How was her suicide "her final test and expression of the Love?"

JANELLE:

1. Who – or what – is Angel?

2. Should the psychotherapeutic process include a friendship between patient and doctor?

MARGEENA:

1. American poet Edna St. Vincent Millay (1892-1950) wrote: *My candle burns at both ends/It will not last the night:/but, ah, my foes, and, oh, my friends/ It gives a lovely light.* What does she mean by this and do you agree?

2. What does the author mean when she states "her light would *not* go out?"

HER HOLINESS:

1. Why is she referred to as Her Holiness?

2. Is she holy?

FRIDA:

1. Does this fictional depiction of a Mexican artist bring to mind any other artist – living or dead?

2. Why does Frida re-marry Diego?

BETH:

1. What has contributed to Beth's obesity?

2. Do you like Beth and why?

THE OLD WOMYN:

1. If Tommy was a girl, would he be called a wimp?

FAITH:

1. Did Mother lie to Faith when she told her Daddy would see the castles she built in the sand?

2. Plato speaks of souls "choosing" their lives. Is he correct?

3. What role does Soul have in our lives?

4. Is there a relationship between our Soul and our geography?

5. Is there a relationship between our Soul and our chosen career?

ROSALIND:

1. As Rosalind's mum claims, is complacency trouble?

2. Do spiritual quests require retreating from the world?

MRS. ROUSSEAU:

1. Is Mrs. Rousseau right when she claims: ". . . there is nothing more dangerous than a stupid person?"

2. Why did Mrs. Rousseau tell her story to the Professor?

3. Was Mrs. Rousseau a sinner?

NORA:

1. Why did Francis feel grateful of the possibility of being killed by Nora?

2. Was it kindness that motivated Nora to spare his life?

3. Radical Jews and Christians alike read the Old Testament as depicting revenge as virtuous. Are Nora's feelings of revenge a virtue?

POLLY:

1. Is soldiering a sport?

2. Is there honour or obscenity to dying in battle?

3. Is there honour or obscenity to killing in battle?

CARNIVAL:

1. Given a choice would you be brilliant but short-lived annual or a hearty perennial?

2. Which is more a celebration of life: Halloween or Carnival?

THE OFFENDER:

1. Dr. Dickson based her offender therapy on the philosophy that "what you did was evil – very evil – but *you* are not evil." Are adult, male sex offenders evil?

2. What is intuition as experienced by Dr. Dickson?

MOONPATH:

1. Does the energy of metaphysical Good, Love, and Honest Intellect remain alive after the death of the body?

ARISTOTLE:

1. Is interspecies communication possible?

EMILY:

1. Is Emily's poetry an untethered religion?

2. Can there be religion "free of man-made churches, priests, and superstitions?"

3. What theological trail did Emily blaze?

4. What motivates a womyn such as Emily to seek fame passionately?

MARIA:

1. Why does Maria feign deafness?

Elephantina:

1. What developmental quirk brought Elephantina to her mission of redeeming the sins of man?

Consummation:

1. Is the husband's deceit motivated by love?

2. Does his deceit discredit what appears to be a loving marriage?

Olive:

1. What is the significance of assigning geometric shapes to bodies, minds, and spirits?

Notes

Notes

OTHER BOOKS FROM FRACTAL EDGE PRESS

Reginald Gibbons. *In the Warhouse.* 2004.
Charlie Newman. *words.* 2004
Larry O. Dean. *I Am Spam.* 2004.
Lina ramona Vitkauskas. *Shooting Dead Films With Poets.* 2004.
Beyond the M. C. *Black on White.* 2004.
Tom Roby. *Griever's Circuit.* 2004.
Maureen Tolman Flannery. *A Fine Line.* 2004.
Billy Tuggle. *Conscience Under Pressure.* 2004.
Ray McNiece. *DIS: Voices from a Shelter.* 2004.
Ray McNiece. *Us? Talking Across America.* 2004.
Gary Copeland Lilley. *The Reprehensibles.* 2004.
PolyRhythmic. *Hosts @ Trace: PolyRhythmic.* 2004.
John Starrs. *The Suburban Poems.* 2004.
David Hernandez. *The Urban Poems.* 2004.
Daniel Cleary. *Elegy for James Gerard and Other Poems for the Larger Voice.* 2005.
Beatriz Badikian Gartler. *Old Gloves: A 20th Century Saga.* 2005.
Charlie Newman. *deadmachinecity.* 2005
Jim Coppoc. *Blood, Sex, & Prayer.* 2005.
Joe Roarty. *Choruses I.* 2005.
Michael Brownstein. *What Stone Is.* 2005.
Wayne Allen Jones. *Stone Works.* 2002.
Bernard McCabe & Wayne Allen Jones. *The A Poems.* 2003.
Wayne Allen Jones. *Decades of Rehearsal.* 2004.
Wayne Allen Jones. *The Decalogue.* 2005.
Wayne Allen Jones. *Sight Lines.* 2005.

Fractal Edge Press
PO Box 220586 Chicago, IL 60622-0586
v: 773-793-4095 f: 773-772-3528
http://www.FractalEdgePress.com
FEPedit@FractalEdgePress.com